Why the Sea Is Full of Salt

and Other Vietnamese Folktales

MINH TRAN HUY

Translated by

HARRY AVELING

Silkworm Books

ISBN 978-616-215-136-1
Original title: *Le Lac né en une nuit*
© Actes Sud 2008

This edition is published by Silkworm Books in 2017.

Silkworm Books
104/5 M. 7, Chiang Mai–Hot Road, T. Suthep
Chiang Mai 50200 Thailand
P.O. Box 296, Phra Singh Post Office, Chiang Mai 50000
info@silkwormbooks.com
http://www.silkwormbooks.com

Typeset in Garamond Premier Pro 12 pt. by Silk Type

Printed and bound in Thailand by O. S. Printing House, Bangkok

5 4 3 2 1

Contents

Preface

Minh Tran Huy, born in 1979 at Clamart in the southwestern suburbs of Paris, is a young French author of Vietnamese descent. She has written three prize-winning novels, *La princesse et le pêcheur* (The princess and the fisherman, 2007), *La double vie de Anna Song* (The double life of Anna Song, 2009), and *Voyageur malgré lui* (Reluctant traveler, 2014).

Vietnamese folktales formed an important theme in Tran Huy's first novel. The tale that provided the title is the last story in this present collection, and several other stories were included there as well, such as "The Woman Who Waited" and "Why the Sea Is Full of Salt." These narratives were an integral part of Tran Huy's childhood and her growing sense of identity. When Tran Huy's publisher, Actes Sud, encouraged her to compile an anthology of Vietnamese stories to follow the novel, she was delighted to be able to "gather, select and rewrite some of them in her own way," as she states in the preface to the collection. The original French anthology is entitled *Le lac né en une nuit* (The lake born in one night, 2008). The title for the present anthology is drawn from Tran Huy's children's book, *Comment la mer devint salée,* published by Actes Sud Junior in 2011.

Why the Sea Is Full of Salt provides a broad range of the best known and most loved Vietnamese folktales. They are set in an imaginary landscape—indicated merely by a mountain, a plain, or a river—in which the wider earthly world and human happiness and pain mingle together. The stories tell of inevitable and often impossible loves, the complexities of marriage, joys deeply felt and sometimes quickly lost, commitments and tragic misunderstandings, and the unintended costs of Confucian filial piety. There are occasional benevolent interventions into the physical world by the Buddha, the immortals, good genies, and Taoist sages, but there is also the destructive anger of malicious genies. Tran Huy compares the tales to a cloud in which "everything passes, nothing is substantial," and also to a lake that is "deceptively calm on the surface, mysterious and unfathomable underneath." They do not always achieve a happy ending and in that, she says, they seem to be truer and more profound than many Western folktales.

I am pleased to be able to present these translations to readers of English. In particular, I would like to thank Dr. Thanh-Van Ton-That for introducing me to Minh Tran Huy's work. My thanks too to Susan Offner for her careful reading of the original manuscript and subsequent editorial work.

Harry Aveling
March 16, 2017

1

The Man and the Evil Spirit

In ancient times, the story is told, an evil spirit ruled in absolute mastery over the world. Every field, fertile or barren, hard or soft, mud or clay, was his. He rented his land to a man, in return for gold. The man, however, was unable to keep more than a very small part of the harvest that his efforts had sprouted, grown, and ripened. Plunged in water up to his knees from morning to night, the man cultivated good white rice without complaint, even though he knew he would not be able to have more than a few fistfuls of grain for himself. The spirit truly showed no pity to the man in this regard and his greed continually increased. He merely calculated that completely starving the man would be foolish.

One year when the harvest promised to be exceptional, and the rain and the sun had agreed to allow the rice fields to yield all they could, the man worked with a light heart, knowing that, this time, he would have enough to eat, and even more than he needed. The angry spirit then decided to impose a new law on the man. "From now on," he declared with a very cunning expression on his face, "the terms of our agreement will be as follows. The tops of the plants will be mine, the other end will be yours." The man timidly tried to protest but the spirit harshly replied, "The contract is not negotiable. It will be as I say." And when the time came to pay the spirit, the man gave him bushel after bushel of grain and kept thousands of the useless roots for himself.

Having been reduced to boiling insects and picking berries to sustain himself, and realizing that he would not be able to live for very long with such a routine, the man prayed with all his might for the Buddha to come to his aid. The Buddha heard his cry and came down from heaven to give him advice. "The matter is simple," he said with a peaceful smile. "All you need to do is to grow sweet potatoes and the spirit can have the leaves for his share." The man faithfully obeyed the Buddha. When autumn came the angry spirit almost strangled him. Without disobeying the spirit's edict in any obvious way, the man, whom the spirit had always considered to be his slave, kept the only edible part of the plant while the spirit received merely the withered leaves.

"Do you want to play wicked games?" the evil spirit howled. "Very well. When summer comes, both the tops and the roots of the plants will be mine. You can have all the rest!" And he disappeared in a cloud of fire and cinders, leaving the poor man more desperate than ever.

"O Enlightened One!" the man called out. "This is a terrible outcome for me concerning the tops of the plants and the roots. Whether I cultivate rice or sweet potato, I will die of hunger one way or another. Please come to my aid, I beg you."

The Buddha appeared, moved by the man's tears, and gave him a sack filled with grain. "Sow these and take care of them. You will have nothing to regret."

At the end of the year, when the evil spirit made his visit and demanded his rent, he was again unable to hold back his anger. The man had succeeded in growing corn, from which he kept the bouncing golden brown ears while nothing remained for the spirit but the dead leaves, stalks, and roots—nothing that was of interest to the inhabitants of either heaven or earth.

"I would prefer to let my possessions rest in fallow land than to see myself stripped of what is mine!" the spirit exclaimed in a bad temper. "You can no longer count on me to rent you anything like this again, and you can just do whatever you want to get by and keep yourself alive. It is none of my business!" And he disappeared, making room for the Buddha.

The man carefully listened to the Enlightened One's counsel. "Call the spirit back and make a new agreement with him. Tell him that you are ready to give him everything you control in exchange for almost nothing in return: a piece of land as wide as the circumference of the shadow cast by a single bamboo." Fearing he would be cheated one more time, the spirit refused at first to listen to the proposal.

But his greed was greater. Thinking that he would obtain everything that belonged to the man in exchange for a tiny parcel of his empire, he agreed.

The man then planted a bamboo bush and traced a circle around its shadow on the earth. "What is inside is mine, what is outside is yours," he observed, while the spirit agreed noisily, convinced that things had finally turned to his favor. Not discouraged, the man began to cultivate his tiny plot of land and to care for the bamboo bush, which he never failed to water regularly. Helped by the Buddha, the bush grew very tall and the part of the earth belonging to the man continued to expand further and further. The spirit resolved to use his power over the savage beasts, ordering the serpents, the tigers, and the elephants to attack the man, the hares to ravage his fields, and the rodents to devour his stores.

The Buddha could not long remain deaf to the lamentations of the man, who had been attacked from all quarters. "You only need to make good use of the bamboo," he calmly declared. "Make a bow and arrows to defend yourself and build fences to protect what belongs to you. Your cares will be greatly reduced."

The man did as he was advised and found that everything was good. But the evil spirit refused to be beaten by these measures. Since his strategies had failed, he turned to a frontal attack. He gathered his armies and launched an offensive, sending his spies to find out the man's weaknesses. The demon soldiers left and crossed over the Buddha's path disguised as poor mendicants. They engaged in conversation with the Buddha and returned to the evil spirit convinced that the man feared nothing so much as bowls of cooked rice, hardboiled eggs, cakes, and pieces of fruit. For his part, the Buddha, having seen through their disguises, learned that above all the demons feared garlic, banana leaves, and lime. He informed the man of this immediately.

Once war had been declared, the spirit's armies launched their attack, bombarding the man with bowls of rice and hardboiled eggs. Delighted, he enjoyed the food and gathered the provisions he needed for the long months ahead on the field of battle. For his part, he hurled hundreds of cloves of garlic at the enemy, sowing terror among the evil army, which was forced to retreat. But a second attack soon followed. The demon warriors hurled cakes, which the man happily collected, while lashing his adversaries with dead banana leaves. The demons beat a hasty retreat, uttering cries of pain, leaving the man victorious a second time. Despite everything, the evil spirit succeeded in launching his final assault—fruits and powdered lime flew from one direction and another. You can guess the outcome of the battle. The man was refreshed while his adversaries took flight in complete disarray without ever coming back.

When he returned to offer his surrender, the evil spirit had lost all traces of arrogance. He was silent, and in a whining voice, begged to be spared. To punish him and his henchmen, the Buddha banished them to the eastern ocean. They had once ruled over the earth and now they had no choice but to leave. The Enlightened One permitted them to return to earth to honor their dead three days a year, during the Feast of Tet. That is why, when the New Year approaches, people spread lime on the ground, plant a bamboo bush in front of their homes, and often hang up dry banana leaves. At the same time they beat gongs and bells to remind the evil spirits that they no longer have any right to live on the land.

2

Betel Leaf, Areca Nut, and Lime

Once there were two brothers named Tan and Lang who were the sons of a mandarin. Although they were not twins, they shared a great deal in common. They were handsome, of a loyal disposition, and had generous hearts. They lived happily in the midst of their family, protected from the world by their rank and their father's wealth. Then they became the victims of a fire that deprived them of their parents and their fortune. Stripped of all their resources, living henceforth alone in the world, they went and took refuge with a distant cousin, a pious man named Luu, who took care of them as if they were his own sons. He himself had only a single daughter.

Time passed and the inevitable happened. The child became a woman. She was as sweet as she was beautiful. Her qualities increased as she became older and Luu, who tenderly cared for the orphans whom he had protected, wanted to give her hand to one of them. But he did not know which one to choose and the young woman too could not decide—the young men were as alike as two grains of rice. They were both handsome and virtuous. Whom should he favor? To complicate matters, although Tan and Lang had both fallen under the spell of the young woman, each brother tried to give way to the other and allow him to marry the person he had begun to love. Finally, Luu organized a meal in the hope of deciding between the pair. He prepared rice cooked in lotus leaves and beef rolls with shallots, and ordered his daughter to offer them two bowls but only one set of chopsticks. Without thinking, the younger brother took the chopsticks and offered them to the elder brother, as was his duty. Luu accepted the elder brother as his son-in-law.

Being a loving brother, Lang quickly forgot the sentiments he had begun to feel for the person who had become his sister-in-law. Unfortunately, Tan, who was very happy in the marriage, neglected his younger brother, who suffered greatly as a result. The husband and wife were so close to each other that Lang felt more and more isolated. A misunderstanding caused by Tan's extreme sensitivity aggravated the situation. One evening the two brothers were returning home from the fields very late. The young wife made her way through the darkness, and believing that she was welcoming her husband, rushed up to the younger brother instead. Tan immediately accused his brother of wanting to betray him.

Wounded by the accusation, Lang decided to leave the house without waiting a moment longer. He departed from the village without taking anything with him and walked straight ahead for several days. His sorrow was so great that he almost forgot his fatigue, which increasingly weighed him down. Wandering from one village to another, exhausted by his efforts and hunger, he finally reached a river that he was unable to cross. He sat on the bank, thinking of those whom he had lost, and his sorrow pierced him so violently that he died. Moved by his suffering, the spirits turned him into a rock so that he would not be eaten by savage beasts.

Lang's disappearance made Tan feel sorry because he now understood what had happened and he regretted his selfishness. Tan set out to search for his brother, resolving to find him and bring him home again, and he undertook a long journey, asking the inhabitants of every village if they had seen Lang. The sun beat down on him but Tan refused to rest. After walking for several days, he collapsed by the side of a river, a few paces away from a large round rock that gave off a comforting coolness. Being at the end of his strength, however, he finally succumbed. He was changed into a very tall tree.

His wife, inconsolable at the absence of her husband, in turn followed every trace of the two brothers. She walked and walked, distraught at the lack of news about him, until her legs collapsed beneath her. She had long left behind the last places where people dwelled and she found herself by the bank of a river, very near a beautiful tree that overhung a rock. With one last sigh, she dragged herself to the tree and put her arms around it so that she would not collapse. She wept for a long time, overwhelmed by her grief, and when she died she was changed into a vine that wound itself around the trunk of the tree.

That night, all the inhabitants of the region had the same dream, which told the story of these three young people. The villagers built a temple in their honor with these few words engraved on the pediment: "Brothers together, a faithful married couple."

Several years later, a terrible drought destroyed all the surrounding vegetation. Only the tree and the vine survived, obstinately remaining green despite the heavy sun, even though a desert extended around them. Seeing this marvel, thousands of pilgrims went to the temple to worship the young people who had disappeared. The king, Huong Vuong, himself heard of the miracle. He was visibly moved by the story of these three transformations and consulted his advisors for an explanation. The advisors refused to speak, except for one very old minister, who made this observation. "Sire, it is the custom, when one wishes to know whether certain persons belong to the same family, to collect a little blood from each of the parties and mix it in a bowl. Let us crush a few leaves of the climbing vine, some fruits from the tree, and a fragment of the rock heated until it dissolves into a fine white powder. Perhaps this will give us the answer we seek."

King Huong Vuong followed the minister's advice and ordered the three ingredients to be ground together. The result was a mixture that quickly turned bright red. In the presence of this sign, the cultivation of the tree and the plant, which were given the names areca palm and betel vine, spread throughout the whole of Vietnam.

They became the symbol of married love and brotherly solidarity in memory of the three young people, and the custom developed of chewing betel leaf, areca nut, and a little lime at celebrations and reunions, in the same way that one smokes cigarettes in the West and the hookah in Mediterranean countries.

3
A Cake for Tet

*H*eaven was kind and even surpassed the expectations of the sixth King Huong Vuong by granting him twenty sons. Having so many male heirs was assuredly a blessing, but it also posed a real problem: when the ruler wished to retire and pass the reins of government to one of his sons, he would have the difficult task of choosing one of them to follow him. Should he choose the oldest, as custom required? The strongest? The best general? Or the one who was most respected? After thinking about it, he decided that these criteria were basically not very important. The principal qualities required in a good king were intelligence, a sense of proportion, and commitment to justice.

During the night, a genie appeared to the king in a dream, and inspired him to devise a test that would help him see things more clearly. The next morning he called his twenty sons together and spoke to them in this way: "My dear children, I am becoming old and the country needs a new king. So I have decided to send you throughout the world with the mission of reporting to me about the most delicious foods you find, together, of course, with their recipes. Whoever brings back the best dish will be my heir. And now, go! You have exactly one year to find what will most delight your father's palate."

Not a little disconcerted by the king's idea, the princes wasted no time in putting their affairs in order. Each man departed, accompanied by an escort of his same rank and means, except for the sixteenth son, Prince Lieu, who had lost his mother when he was a very small baby and had neither counselors nor servers at his disposal. With a heavy heart he watched his brothers set out on their journeys, some with a procession of followers, others with an armed guard, and he thought to himself, "How can I explore the world and satisfy my father when I don't even have a horse to ride? It's impossible . . ." He turned the problem over and over again in his mind without finding a solution, and finally fell asleep.

During his sleep, a genie with a long white beard and dressed in yellow silk (the same genie, perhaps, that had appeared to the king) visited him in a dream. "I know how lonely you are and the pious hope that lives in your heart. The throne does not interest you as much as the desire to serve and obey your father. On these grounds, you deserve my assistance. There is no need to gallop off to exotic lands to report precious foods, for, truth be told, there is nothing better than the rice that has sustained human beings for all eternity.

13

It is enough to take some glutinous rice, clean it with the purest water, and steam it. When it is ready, knead it into two cakes. You should make the first one round, like the dome of the sky—it will be a tribute to the benefits that heaven gives mankind. As for the second, make it square as a symbol of the earth that nourishes all people. You can fill the insides of the cakes with a mixture of crushed haricot beans, onions, and pork mixed with various kinds of fat. Wrap them all up in banana leaves and cook them in an oven for a whole day and night. Try it several times so you know that the recipe will succeed, and your efforts will surely be well rewarded."

When the prince woke up, he went and told it to the old nurse who had taken care of him after his mother died. "The dream is a sign from heaven. Heaven will protect you, my child. You must do as it has said." Reassured by these words, Lieu gathered the necessary ingredients and practiced making the cakes. He spent several weeks learning how to cook the glutinous rice, deciding how long it should take and the right temperature to use, as well as the best quantities of lard and bean paste. Finally he had a perfect recipe. Then he armed himself with the virtue of patience, and in accordance with the genie's advice, calmly waited for the end of the period that the king had decreed.

On the set day, the princes flooded in to the court, bringing unnamed delicacies back from their travels. Their servants wore red and gold livery and carried silver platters filled with the most exotic and delicate foods ever seen in the kingdom. Rare fruits, spices with subtle aromas, fish from distant oceans, foods cooked with exquisite refinement—the king's table was covered with the most fabulous dishes, one after another. Only Lieu stayed in the background, his cakes in his hands. No one paid any attention to him in the presence of such an abundance of marvels. The king tasted each plate with delight, his eyes shining and his nostrils quivering. Peacock rolls, phoenix paté, bear cub paws, rhinoceros liver . . . what fragrances, what colors, what artistic arrangements, what unexpected combinations! Fresh or roasted, bitter or sweet and salted, solid or light as air, the innumerable dishes placed before the king seemed to make his choice more difficult than ever.

It was finally Lieu's turn to show what he had discovered. The old ruler curiously unwrapped the humble parcel of banana leaves and took a mouthful of the first cake and then the second cake. He closed his eyes to taste the mix of flavors, then opened them again. His pupils shone. He stood up to announce that the competition had come to an end and that he could proclaim the undeniable winner, the man who would succeed him on the throne.

"My beloved sons," he declared, "I would like to thank you for all the trouble you have undertaken to report to me about all the countries in the world you have visited to bring me the strangest and most succulent dishes that there are. But, to be honest, how could you ever cook them again, seeing that you could not possibly find all of the ingredients in this country? Not only are Lieu's cakes delicious, the ingredients are easy to obtain. Moreover, in making one cake round and the other square, he has united both the spiritual and the physical. He not only wanted to honor the palace but he also sought to pay tribute to heaven and earth, to which we owe everything. From all these points of view, he deserves to be my successor."

Bowing down, the young prince began to speak. "Father, I do not deserve any of the praise you have given me. I can lay no claim to having discovered the recipe for these cakes." Then he told the king and all who were present there about the advice he had received from the genie.

"I respect your honesty, my son," the king replied. "And it only strengthens my conviction that you are worthy to rule the kingdom. This divine intervention, which has shown you heaven's favor, is brilliant proof of that." He ordered the recipe to be distributed throughout the land, and decreed that the round cake should bear the name *banh day* and the square cake should be called *banh chung*. And as he had promised, he gave his authority to Prince Lieu, who ascended to the throne and became the seventh Hoang king.

Since then, each New Year, everyone in Vietnam cooks glutinous rice buns to celebrate the feast of Tet, especially *banh chung*, the symbol of our gratitude to the earth that nourishes us.

4
Why the Sea Is Full of Salt

A very long time ago, there were two brothers who lived in a small fishing village. Except for their ties of blood, they had nothing in common. The older brother, Seo, was a hard man whose face displayed the marks of a jealous and hypocritical nature. He had tiny eyes and a tight mouth. He loved nothing more than being cruel to his younger brother. The younger brother, Tam, was as pure in his behavior as he was in his heart, and his vigorous appearance, his friendly manners, were the opposite in every possible way to those of his brother.

At that time, the sea was sweet and you could dive into it with your eyes wide open in order to observe the corals and the fish that spun about in the clear water. Salt cost more than jade and Seo and Tam led a meager existence based on the results of their fishing, which they sold or bartered for clothing and other extremely basic necessities. Rising at dawn, they spent the whole day in their boats, busily casting their nets and setting lines, then returning home exhausted at nightfall. They had lost their mother while they were still small boys and lived with their father, who was always ready to accompany them and help them with their various tasks.

One day, weakened by his advanced years, the old man was attacked by a severe illness nobody could cure. On his deathbed, he called his sons and gave them some final words of advice. "Be wise enough not to want more than you can have, always behave in an honest way, and be loyal brothers. Soon you will be on your own in the world. Strive to remember that your family is the most precious possession you have." And with these words, he died.

Grief almost shattered Tam's heart, but Seo was the absolute master of his own emotions. Pretending concern for his brother, Seo divided the meager possessions left by their father. Without any regard for the last wishes of the man who had raised them, he abused his younger brother's trust and deceitfully seized the best nets, the strongest boat, and the family home, from which he banished his brother. There was nothing left for Tam but a worn-out net, a leaky boat, and a few fishing lines. Nevertheless, Tam did not criticize his brother, and he forced himself to live simply with what Seo had been willing to leave to him.

Although life was hard, Tam was not overwhelmed by his sufferings. In spite of his weariness, he never failed to honor his father's memory, regularly placing offerings at the ancestors' altar he had built near his straw hut. One evening, when he was particularly weary, he had an extraordinary dream. A very kind-looking old man appeared, dressed in a silk robe, and spoke these words. "My dear child, I have been watching you for a long time. Your virtues are innumerable and your conduct is exemplary, but you have always been badly rewarded. So I have decided to give you a gift." He took a woven straw basket out from his sleeve. "This is no ordinary basket," he declared. "All you have to do is bow three times in front of it and recite these words: 'O threefold venerated Master of the Salt, honor me with your blessings,' and it will fill with salt. When you have enough, bow three times again and say: 'O Master of the Salt, this is enough. I thank you a thousand times over.' And the supply of salt will stop. Do you understand?" Tam nodded and expressed his gratitude. "It's nothing. Make good use of the basket and be happy." And with a smile, the genie vanished.

The day after his dream, Tam found a basket near the head of his bed, exactly as he had dreamed. He took it and, following the genie's instructions, had all the salt he wanted. That was the end of his poverty. Thousands of people came to buy their provisions from him because he sold salt at a very low price and even gave it away when he thought this was necessary. His reputation as a just and generous man grew, as did his fortune. Soon he was able to repair his nets, buy a new boat, and enlarge his house, painting the walls with white lime.

As for Seo, he was unable to contain his anger when he was confronted with this sudden prosperity. "How can this be possible? I left this wretch almost nothing to live on and now look! He is much richer than I am." But hiding his real feelings behind a mask of goodwill, he went to pay a visit to Tam, hoping that he might discover his secret. He didn't need to look for very long. At the first mention, the young man told him in a straightforward way about meeting the old man and the magic formula for making salt. At the same time Tam invited Seo to stay with him for as long as he liked. Completely overwhelmed by his own jealousy, Seo accepted the invitation in the hope of stealing the treasure.

Night came. As soon as Tam was peacefully asleep, Seo began to ransack the house. He finally found the wooden box containing the genie's gift and fled in his boat without taking any other luggage, confident that he would be able to establish himself wherever he wanted, thanks to the basket. He weighed anchor holding the precious object close to his body, and once he was well out in the open, gave way to his desire to invoke the Master of the Salt. He bowed three times and recited the spell: "O threefold venerated Master of the Salt, honor me with your blessings." Immediately salt gushed out. Seo gave a cry of joy and watched happily as the grains filled the basket, then overflowed and covered the boards of the deck with a fine white powder.

"That's fine, you can stop," he called out. But his words had no effect. "That's fine, I said!" he repeated anxiously. The deck was completely buried and the weight of the salt threatened to sink the boat. Overcome by fear, Seo began to scream, "Stop, that's plenty, you are going to drown us all!" He recited all sorts of spells, both cursed and begged the basket, but all in vain. The basket continued spitting out salt until it covered Seo's body, his goods, his boat, and his greed.

5
The First Mosquito

Do you know where mosquitoes come from, those creatures that now swarm all over Vietnam? A legend explains that they were born in very particular circumstances. It all began with a poor peasant couple. The man, named Ngoc Tam, was the kindest and greatest of incarnated souls. He adored his wife, Nhan Diep, whose beauty had bewitched him from the first time he saw her—to such an extent that he treated her like a queen rather than a wife. He accepted each word she spoke as if it were the absolute truth, obeyed the least of her gestures immediately, and spared no effort to ensure that she led a comfortable life. When she expressed a wish for something, he considered it an order and rushed to fulfill her desires. Blinded by his feelings, he could not see that although he adored her, she had simply chosen him because there was no one better on offer. She dreamed of silken robes and jewels, servants and grand mansions, a life of leisure and sloth far removed from the virtuous ideal her husband cultivated.

Gnawed by a dissatisfaction that for better or worse she forced herself to hide, Nhan Diep finally died, as if she had been worn away from the inside. Her death almost drove Ngoc Tam mad. Inconsolable, he refused to accept the fact, and rather than bury the body of his dearly beloved wife, he decided to keep her nearby him and not to concern himself with anything else. Deaf to the admonitions of his family and friends, he drifted about with Nhan Diep's coffin on a sampan, weeping day and night over his misfortune, only going ashore to pick fresh flowers and piously place them on the floating tomb.

He was as incapable of resting as he was of eating properly and was soon little more than skin on bone. He had almost completely lost his mind when one day his boat ran aground on an unknown beach at the foot of a tall leafy mountain. The grass was thick, there was an abundance of fruit and flowers, the sun shone brightly on the particles of dust floating in the air, and the atmosphere was filled with the singing of a thousand birds.

"Did I die while I was sleeping? Have I gone to heaven?" Ngoc Tam asked himself. "This land is far too beautiful not to be enchanted." Then he saw an old man with a beard and hair as white as snow advancing towards him, whose black and lively eyes nevertheless seemed witness to his eternal youthfulness.

"Welcome, my son. I know your merits and do not want to allow such virtue to perish in vain. Therefore I directed your boat towards my lands so that I could invite you to become one of my disciples. If you follow me, I will teach you the properties of every medicinal plant, how to make potions and medicines capable of curing even the most severe and difficult diseases, and you will be able to use this knowledge to make a good livelihood treating your fellow human beings."

On hearing these words, Ngoc Tam recognized the genie of mountains who was capable of curing every illness, and he threw himself to the ground. "O genie! I thank you a thousand times over for your generosity and I beg your pardon. To be truthful, I do not want to travel through this world without my wife. Without her, I am no more than a shadow of my former self. My existence has no meaning and there is only one thing I want: for my wife to return to life. If you can do it, I beseech you to revive her."

The old man cast a thoughtful glance towards Ngoc Tam as he kneeled before him. "Are you sure of yourself? Only study and meditation can allow a man to fulfill his destiny by detaching himself from the illusions of the world. Mortal joys are frivolous and transitory, and nothing is more vain, frivolous, or fallible than the ties of the flesh." However, Ngoc Tam was so persistent that the genie was finally swayed by his prayers. "Since you insist, I will show you the way to bring your wife back to your side. Prick your finger and let three drops of blood fall onto your wife's lips. She will wake up again as if she has just been asleep for a long time."

It was no sooner said than done. Having swallowed the three drops of blood, Nhan Diep opened her eyes and sat up as if nothing had happened. "Where are we, my dear husband? What has happened? I seem to have had a very strange dream."

"It was not a dream," the genie replied. "You crossed over the River of the Dead, and without your husband you would have remained there forever. Never forget what you owe to his devotion!"

The couple acknowledged their gratitude to the genie before setting out to return home. They stopped at a small port and Ngoc Tam went ashore to find new provisions while Nhan Diep lazed about, amusing herself exploring the alleys and sights, all the while protecting her skin from the ravages of the sun. Admiring the young woman's beauty, a rich merchant tied up his boat near to her own. He engaged her in conversation and invited her to take tea with him. "It will also be an opportunity to show you such fabrics as you have never seen before—silk brocades, embroidered satins, damascened velvets, and bands of gold and silver!" he promised her. Nhan Diep could not long resist his honeyed words and she went up onto the craft. While she was lost in her admiration of the riches displayed by the merchant, he gave the order to weigh anchor.

The boat flew like the wind and when Ngoc Tam returned to his boat he could do nothing but weep a second time over the disappearance of his wife. Informed of what had happened by those who had witnessed the abduction, he spent a whole month crisscrossing the waters before finding Nhan Diep. The young woman was standing on a wharf, wearing a magnificent dress made of crimson silk. A band of gold and jade held her hair in place and her ears and neck were decorated with pearls.

Seeing her husband coming towards her dressed in rags, Nhan Diep turned pale. She smiled disdainfully at his exhaustion from having searched so hard for her. Very satisfied with the life of pleasure and luxury she was leading, she ungraciously refused his appeals. She made him clearly understand that she had never loved him and that he had been nothing but the least worse choice available to her at that time. "I am happy and I have absolutely no intention of returning to a life of poverty with you. Don't ask me, just go away, unless you want my servants to beat you!" Her tone gave him no room for any reply.

For the first time, Ngoc Tam understood what sort of a person Nhan Diep really was. She had shown her true colors, and the insolence and selfishness of her character were too obvious for him to be deceived any further. He was henceforth cured of the love he had borne for a woman who, he understood that day, had nothing in common with the person he was looking at. So he replied calmly, "Do you want to be free? Very well. I have only one condition: return the three drops of blood I gave you. I don't want you to carry the slightest bit of me in your body."

Happy to have made such a good bargain, Nhan Diep took a knife and made a slight cut in her finger. But as soon as the third drop fell, her cheeks lost their color and she toppled to the ground. All attempts to revive her failed. She was dead.

However, her greedy soul was unable to leave the world. Nhan Diep was reincarnated in the form of a tiny insect that continually tormented Ngoc Tam by buzzing about his ears, uttering prayers, excuses, and other declarations of her remorse. She persistently tried to sting him and take back the three drops of blood required for her restoration. Time passed, the species multiplied, and the descendants of the first mosquito continue this very day to harass humankind and suck their blood.

6
The Shadow of the Father

There was once a peasant couple who lived in a small village. They led a simple but happy life and they were waiting for their first child when the man was called up into the army. He was forced to go to fight at the front, leaving his family to live as best they could in the clay hut he had built with his own hands. The baby arrived on time, ten days after his father's departure, and the mother raised him on her own, not without some difficulty. She worked in the rice fields every day and at the same time took on many small jobs in order to provide for their needs. She only had the nighttime to be with her little boy.

Several autumns passed and there was no news of her husband. The child began to babble his first words and soon began to ask for his father. She did not know what to tell him. One night, a fierce thunderstorm howled and the little one, terrified, held tightly to his mother and began to cry. Lighting a small oil lamp that sat at the head of her bed, the mother pointed to her shadow projected onto the wall opposite them. "Don't be afraid, darling. Look, your father is there, watching over us." Reassured, the child immediately dried his tears. His mother showed him how to join his hands and bow to his father. From then on, not a day passed without her lighting the lamp for the child to see the shadow and bow down before he went to bed. It became a ritual the son willingly accepted, happy to see that they were no longer alone.

After a number of years, the war ended and the husband returned home. Overjoyed at their being together again, the wife decided to honor her husband's return. She went to the market to buy some provisions to offer the ancestors and prepare a feast. While she was gone, the child babbled away and the man decided to teach him some manners. He was offended when the boy refused to call him father.

"You are not my father," the little boy retorted. "My father comes to pay us a visit every evening, I bow down to him before I go to bed and he sleeps with my mother." The man inevitably misunderstood the remarks. He concluded from these innocent words that his wife had taken a lover while he was away risking his life at the front.

When the woman returned from the market with a smile on her lips, she told him that she wanted to make an offering to the ancestors. The man replied with an icy silence. Struck by his somber mood, she did not dare to speak and uttered not a single word more. He was too proud to ask her anything, and later, although he burned to be proven wrong, he kept his suspicions to himself. However, his actions spoke for him: he unrolled the mat prior to their prayers before the altar, bowed repeatedly, and then, when it was his wife's turn, deliberately rolled up the mat again, without leaving her time to pray. She looked at him sadly but did not utter a word of reproach. The woman set out three bowls and three pairs of chopsticks, then served the steaming rice. The husband allowed the rice to grow cold while his wife fed the child. She could hardly breathe. Finally, he left the table, and with his bag on his back, crossed over the threshold and never came back.

His incomprehensible behavior almost drove the woman mad. She waited for her husband for some time, hoping that he would return and explain his actions. But the days passed and she heard no news. Eventually the pain of his abandoning her without even explaining why became intolerable. She went to the bank of the river and drowned herself.

The news of her death reached the man. Filled with remorse he decided to return to his village and look after his son. Evening having fallen, he lit the wick of the oil lamp in order to have a little light. Imagine his surprise when he saw the boy join his hands together and bow to his shadow, calling it father.

He understood everything. It was too late, unfortunately, to correct his catastrophic error. The man could only build a temple in memory of the woman who had loyally fulfilled her duties. He forced himself to be a good father, remaining faithful for the rest of his life to the woman he had unfairly accused.

7

Tam and Cam

There was once a wealthy peasant couple who owned vast and fertile fields that produced much more rice than they could ever hope to eat. They had one daughter, Tam, meaning "broken rice," who was as sweet as she was lovely. The three of them lived peacefully together until the day the mother suddenly died of some unknown illness. Thinking that Tam needed a mother, the house needed a woman at its center, and he needed a wife who could give him a son, the father eventually remarried.

At first, everything went well and the new wife showed herself to be very amiable. But the situation changed completely when she brought a daughter into the world named Cam, or "rice chaff." From then on, the stepmother was only interested in her own daughter. She made Tam do all the chores—sweeping, cooking, and washing clothes. The couple obtained even more fields. The father, at the end of his strength, quickly joined his first wife in the grave, leaving his daughter to the mercy of her cruel stepmother, who endlessly persecuted her.

The years passed and only one person worked in this house to take care of the others. Their resources gradually dwindled and they exhausted their wealth. While the stepmother continued to praise Cam and care for all her needs, Tam was treated more like a servant than a daughter. However, despite her rags, her lack of nourishment, and the bad treatment she received, Tam was the most beautiful of the three. Her eyes sparkled and her skin was like silk while her half sister grew uglier each day, to the mother's annoyance.

One fine morning, the stepmother ordered her young girls to go fishing in a nearby river that was flooded, as happened at certain seasons, and swarming with fish and shrimps. She promised them, "I will give a prize to whomever brings me the best catch—a pretty red blouse!" The young ladies left together but as soon as they arrived at their destination, behaved in completely opposite ways. Tam waded in the water up to the middle of her thighs and searched through the mud of the river, despite the sun and the stiffling heat. Cam lay down under the shade of the tall trees that lined the riverbank, strolled along the riverside, and played with the birds and the butterflies.

By the time the morning was over, Tam had filled her basket to overflowing, while Cam's remained empty. But the lazy wretch was not content just to avoid hours of hard work. She still coveted the blouse as much as ever. So she shouted, "Oh, my sister, plunging your hands into the mud has made your neck and face dirty. You must go and wash yourself. Otherwise, our mother will punish you. Use the water from that well over there." Unsuspecting, Tam walked towards the well. When she returned, her basket was empty. Cam had emptied its contents into her own basket and quickly set off for home.

Utterly distraught, Tam sat on the riverbank and wept with all her heart. It was then that the Buddha appeared to her. "Why are you so sad, my child?" he gently asked. And when Tam, who was momentarily surprised, told him of her troubles, he said, "Dry your tears and look at the bottom of your basket. There is still something there." The young girl discovered a tiny fish hidden in the weave of the bamboo basket. "Put it in the lotus pond of the village pagoda and keep a few grains of your rice for it every day. Call the fish by singing these words, 'Golden goby, silver goby, rise up and eat my rice, reject the bad grain and cold soup that others may offer you.' The fish will come and find you. Tell him your troubles and he will be a great comfort to you." Having given her this advice, the Buddha disappeared.

From then on, Tam had a friend whom she fed every night before going to bed. She told him everything that happened to her, and this consoled her for the difficult life she led. The mistress of the house was astonished by the young girl's good humor, which made her more beautiful than ever, and she ordered Cam to spy on Tam and follow her when she went out so as to be able to discover her secret. Accordingly, when night fell, Cam, hiding behind a pillar, saw her half sister call the goby and tell him what had happened during the day. Cam rushed off to describe the scene to her mother. The next day, the stepmother sent Tam to take a message to a distant village. Then, accompanied by her daughter, she summoned the goby by chanting the spell.

As soon as the fish surfaced, the two women caught it, then grilled and ate it. When Tam returned and waited in front of the lotus pond, her calls were in vain. A few drops of blood floated to the surface. She understood what had happened and burst into tears. Again the Buddha appeared to her. "Do not cry, my child," he said. "If you look on the ground beneath the bamboo fence, you will find the remains of your goby. Put the bones in a clay pot, bury them near your mother's grave, and don't worry any more." Tam dug in the dirt, gathered the fish bones, and followed the Buddha's advice.

Some time later the whole village was preparing to celebrate the spring festival. They were expecting a visit from the king and innumerable spectacles had all been announced to celebrate the event, including concerts, minstrels, and water puppets. Because the occasion was to be so wonderful, Tam hoped that her stepmother would allow her to accompany her. When the moment came to leave, the mistress of the house led Tam to a huge heap of grain. "I don't see any difficulty in your attending the celebrations," she said with a sarcastic smile. "I only ask that before you join us you separate the rice from the husks."

Leaving the young girl with this impossible task, she called Cam, made up her face, applied perfume, and dressed her in the most beautiful clothes to add to her enjoyment at the festivities. Just as poor Tam was left with tears of despair running down her face, the Buddha came towards her. "Stop crying, my child. The sparrows will come and help you."

"The sparrows?" the young girl asked. "But won't they eat every last grain?"

"Don't worry," the Buddha reassured her, "just watch."

He had no sooner spoken than the air hummed with the beating of thousands of wings. Vast numbers of birds flew over the heap of grain and in a few minutes the rice and the chaff had been carefully separated.

Tam's joy was short lived. She quickly realized that she had nothing to wear except for her rags. Once more the Buddha swept away her worries. "Go and dig up the pot you buried near your mother's grave. You will find everything you need there." The young girl went and dug in the soft ground for the pot, and to her amazement, instead of the goby bones there were clothes, jewels, and the most beautiful ornaments. She chose a pair of silk trousers, an embroidered blouse, and a pair of slippers decorated with phoenixes and sparkling all over with tiny sapphires. And as she wondered how to get to the festivities without dragging these magnificent garments through the dust along the highways, she spotted a tiny pony at the bottom of the pot, which, as soon as she put it on the ground, grew to become a superb stallion with a golden harness. She sat in the saddle and the animal took her to witness the arrival of the royal procession.

As soon as she appeared, the admiring villagers made way for her to pass, believing that they were dealing with a woman of high position. When Cam saw her, she frowned and tugged at her mother's sleeve. "Mother, Mother, she looks like Tam," she whispered into her mother's ear. "What do you think?"

"What are you saying, my daughter?" the woman replied. "It's impossible, just look at her. How could that little slut have found the means to dress like this?" On hearing them, Tam panicked and pulled back on the horse's reins so hard that she lost one of her slippers in the river. The royal elephant, which was just beginning to cross the river, stopped immediately and trumpeted loudly, obstinately refusing to take another step forwards.

"Something is stopping the elephant from moving ahead," the king announced. "Guards, search the river bed!" After a few minutes of searching, they brought him a beautiful embroidered slipper decorated with clusters of precious stones. The ruler turned the slipper over and over in admiration, and then had his heralds announce that he would marry the woman who owned the shoe. Hundreds of candidates presented themselves but none of them fitted the slipper. The royal eunuch, with his piercing gaze, then noticed Tam, who was gracefully leaning against a tree trying to hide her bare foot under her robe. Wading through the crowd, he demanded that she try the slipper. It fitted her perfectly.

Enchanted by her beauty, the king happily reaffirmed his promise. The sweetness and wisdom of his bride won him over immediately.

Inwardly raging, Cam and her mother were forced to hide their jealousy beneath the sweetest words, which easily deceived the young woman. The wedding was celebrated with sumptuous feasting, and Tam took up residence in the palace, where she lived in peace and contentment by the side of the king.

Some time later, however, Tam asked to be allowed to return to her village to celebrate the anniversary of her father's death. She took a number of magnificent gifts with her, but the sly stepmother suggested, "My dear daughter, I thank you for your generosity. But don't you think that the Buddha would be more appreciative of something less luxurious, perhaps something straight from your heart? Climb the areca palm as you used to, and pick some nuts." Tam immediately did so. Cam and the stepmother waited until she had reached the top of he palm, and then began attacking the base of the tree with axes.

"What are you doing?" Tam asked.

"Nothing to worry about," the stepmother replied. "Some red ants are climbing on the areca palm and we are hitting them to make sure that they don't bite you." And they continued cutting the trunk even more vigorously. Once they had hacked well into the palm, the trunk finally broke, and with a terrible cracking sound, fell into the deep waters of a nearby pond, where poor Tam drowned.

The stepmother immediately dressed her daughter in the clothes of the deceased girl and sent her to the court with the message that as the queen had died in a terrible accident, her sister had come to take her place, as was the custom, hoping to ease the sorrow of the king. Overwhelmed by his grief, the king allowed Cam to stay.

One day when he was walking in his garden, an oriole with golden feathers appeared from nowhere and perched on an apple tree. It began to sing. The king recognized the tune as one that his deceased wife was fond of and he called out, "Oh oriole, dear oriole, if you are the incarnate soul of my wife, please come and take refuge in the sleeve of my gown!" The bird immediately flew down and the king could not restrain his joy. He ordered a craftsman to build a huge cage of pure gold, and he looked after the bird himself, feeding his new favorite with ripe grain and clean water. He spent every moment of his leisure time with the bird, listening to it sing hour after hour.

This friendship profoundly annoyed Cam and she went to her mother. She was told what to do and obeyed the instructions to the letter. While the king was away visiting a distant province, she grabbed the oriole and held it tightly until she strangled it. Then she buried the remains in a corner of the garden and told the king that nobody had been able to stop a cat from pouncing on the bird and carrying it away. With a heavy heart, the king had no choice but to accept her explanations.

Now a magnificent flamboyant tree soon grew on the spot where the oriole had been buried. The king, attracted by the tree, quickly became used to resting in its shade because he only had to close his eyes and the smiling image of his dearly beloved would appear at once. This too provoked Cam's jealousy. First the king had preferred a bird to her, and now he was more interested in a tree! The mother, when asked, told her, "Cut down the flamboyant tree on the pretext that you need some wood to make a loom." Cam obeyed. But as soon as she started to weave cloth, she heard the shuttle murmur, "You have stolen your sister's husband. Your sister will tear out your eyes!" Terrified, she burned the loom and threw away the cinders far from the palace.

At the spot where she had thrown the cinders, an imposing persimmon tree soon grew, and before long all the other trees sheltered beneath its branches. People passing by admired the persimmon, and an old lady who sold rice cakes and tea had an idea to set up her bamboo stall right under the tree. She was good, kind, and always had a smile on her lips. People soon grew used to chatting with her for a few minutes as they drank tea and chewed on her cakes, protected from the sun by the leaves of the persimmon tree.

One evening, as she was gathering her goods and preparing to fold up her stall, a delicious fragrance tickled her nose. She looked up and saw an enormous piece of fruit of an appetizing yellow color, sitting enthroned alone at the top of the tree. The perfume was intoxicating, but she was too old to climb the tree and pick the fruit. So she vowed, "Oh persimmon, beautiful persimmon, please drop into my sack. I won't eat you, I promise. I just want to smell you." Straightaway the fruit fell into her basket and the lady took it home. She placed her treasure on a piece of furniture near her bed.

Soon strange things began to happen. Each day when she came home from work, the old lady found that her house had been tidied and swept, and a hot meal was waiting on the table. Keen to solve this mystery, she pretended to leave one morning with her stall under her arm, but then surreptitiously returned. She saw a very beautiful young woman emerge from the piece of fruit, then sweep the humble lodgings. Completely amazed, she opened the door and put her arms around the girl. The old lady was very moved, and warmly thanking her, asked her who she was. Tam, because it was indeed her, told her about her life and her successive reincarnations, explaining that she had finally been transformed into a fairy and sent into the world to help the old lady, whose virtues had come to the attention of heaven. The woman begged her to retain her true form. "Stay with me in this body. Then I will have an adopted daughter." Tam agreed and broke the skin around the fruit. The two women opened a small inn in the village. The establishment quickly became famous. Travelers praised its friendliness, its food, and most of all, Tam's gracefulness.

It came to pass one night that the king, who was traveling incognito, decided to make a stopover at the inn. The old lady brought him a tray with some tea, some areca nuts, and a few quids of betel. When he saw this, the king leapt up, greatly disturbed. "My late wife used to roll betel leaves in the shape of phoenix wings, grandmother. Where did you learn to do this?"

"Have you seen my poor hands, my lord? I can't undertake such a delicate task these days. My daughter does it for me." She then summoned Tam, who had been listening behind the curtain that separated the kitchen from the main room. The girl stepped forward.

The king was as happy as he was surprised—enormously so, in both cases. The young woman told him about the torments she had endured, and he took her back to the palace before calling Cam.

When Cam saw that the couple had been reunited, the color drained from her face, but being obliged to show her joy at her sister's return, she had to hide her displeasure for better or worse. "What a delight to see you again, my dear sister. And looking more beautiful than ever! How do you keep your skin looking so fresh?"

"Nothing could be simpler," Tam calmly replied. "When you bathe, prepare a pot of boiling water. Then pour it over yourself and you will be as white as milk." Impatiently, Cam followed these directions and died in terrible pain. Tam ordered the body to be cut into pieces, seasoned, and thrown into a little brine, before packing them in a little basket and sending them to her stepmother as a gift. The woman was delighted. "Truth to tell, not even my own daughter looks after me this well!" And she ate the meat, which she found to be delicious.

Being a connoisseur, she became accustomed to nibbling the delicacy each day. When she reached the end of her supply, her gaze fell onto a dark mass floating at the bottom of the pot. "What is this?" she thought with disgust. "It almost seems like the animal's fur." Plunging her hand into the pot, she pulled out Cam's head, and screaming with horror, threw herself into the river that ran just below her house.

8

The Magic Crossbow

Over two thousand years ago Vietnam was divided into many states. The story is told that, in this distant era, a prince of the Thuc kingdom fell madly in love with a princess from Van Lang. Alas! His demand that she marry him was rejected. Mad with anger and unrequited love, he waged a merciless war against Van Lang. He sought revenge for the rest of his life, and even his death did not put an end to the conflict. From one generation to the next, battles and truces followed each other, and the cycle did not end with the arrival of King An Duong Vuong, who united the two countries under the name of Au Lac.

Keen to confirm his power and to protect his lands against invaders, An Duong Vuong decided to erect an enormous citadel, with guard towers at regular distances, deep moats, and surrounding fortified walls placed one behind the other in the form of a snail. The citadel took its name from this arrangement—Co Lua, "City of the

Conch." The work advanced at great speed and the workers were able to raise the ramparts in only a few weeks, to the great satisfaction of the king. His joy did not last long, unfortunately. One night the walls trembled of their own accord, then collapsed in just a few seconds. The carefully erected buildings were no more than ruins. Refusing to accept this state of affairs, the king immediately ordered the work to be resumed. The workers undertook this task three times in all, and their efforts proved to be in vain three times as well.

That the same phenomenon should repeat itself in this way seemed inexplicable, and An Duong Vuong decided to appeal to heaven. He erected an altar, placed offerings there with his own hands, and immersed himself in prayer for several days. One night, an old man with white hair around his head and a peaceful look on his face appeared to him in a dream. "I know that above all you want peace, not war," he declared. "For that reason, I will help you. At dawn tomorrow, go to the edge of the ocean and you will meet an envoy from the Tranquil Waters. Only he can allow you to build your citadel."

As soon as he opened his eyes, King An Duong Vuong quickly dressed and set out for the shore, eagerly looking out for his savior. A bright spot soon appeared on the horizon. The sun was feeble by comparison. Its rays were less resplendent than the object that the king, dazzled, identified as the shell of an enormous golden tortoise. Her large flippers cut though the water in a way that was both easy and rapid, and she spoke to An Duong Vuong in a human voice.

"I am an envoy sent from the Tranquil Waters. My name is Kim Qui, and I am a genie in the form of a golden tortoise. Your prayers have been heard and I have come to assist you." The king bowed down as a sign of respect. "The reason your citadel walls keep falling is because the evil spirits who live in the mountains continually provoke the ghosts of the enemies you have vanquished and they are eager for revenge. It is difficult to chase them away but not impossible. First you must kill their chief, who has taken the form of a white cock belonging to an innkeeper resident at the foot of the mountains, several hundred meters away from here. Then you must gather your troops and order them to hide around the cabin you will see there, which appears to be empty. When night comes, the demons take on various physical forms and camp there. That is the only time they are vulnerable. Your soldiers will be able to shoot them full of arrows. If everything goes well, the demons will be forced to beat a retreat and they will never again oppose the building of your citadel."

Everything proceeded as the genie advised. Once the demons had been put to flight, the builders returned to their work and the city rose, tall and proud, surrounded by its fortified walls. Her task completed, Kim Qui decided to leave. Saddened by the tortoise's departure, King An Duong Vuong accompanied her to the shore, thanking her profusely, and observing, "Through your grace, I have been able to successfully complete this task and protect my people. But these ramparts will never be sufficient to discourage invaders. How will we be able to defend ourselves when you are no longer here?"

The genie in the form of a golden tortoise kindly replied, "I know that you are only interested in the welfare of your country. Whether empires live in peace or not depends on the will of heaven, but equally on that of men as well. So I will give you a gift." She then tore off one of her claws and offered it to the king. "Shape this claw to become the trigger for your crossbow. Each time you fire an arrow, not just one enemy soldier but thousands will lose their lives." An Duong Vuong gratefully accepted the gift and prostrated on the ground. "Never forget that you and only you are responsible for the security of your kingdom. Your army cannot lighten the burden of your responsibility. You must continually be aware of your duty." And with these words, the golden tortoise returned to the open sea.

An Duong Vuong immediately ordered his most skilled craftsmen to make a crossbow fit for the sacred claw and engrave a symbol of the golden tortoise on the shining hardwood of the bow. But many years passed before he had the opportunity to use it. For a long time, Au Lac knew nothing but peace and prosperity. The inhabitants worked hard, lush rice fields stretched farther than the eye could see, and the mandarins administrated their regions wisely under the careful supervision of An Duong Vuong, whose wisdom and intelligence inspired respect everywhere.

When he heard about the splendor of Au Lac, Tan Thuy Hoang, the emperor of China, decided to annex the kingdom in order to increase his own wealth. He placed General Trieu Da at the head of an army of five hundred thousand men, who surged down from the Mountain of the Rusty Axe to attack the walls around Au Lac. This sea of furious warriors, covered from head to toe in metal armor, bearing swords and sharp spears, scarcely worried An Duong Vuong at all. He climbed the stairs in the highest tower of the citadel, four at a time, to where he had hidden the sacred crossbow. Raising the golden tortoise's gift, he fired three arrows. Thirty thousand Chinese corpses crashed to the ground, while the other soldiers, terrified, fled.

No army, not even the most powerful in the world, would have been able to fight against such a phenomenon. Trieu Da decided to try a trick. Pretending to surrender, he sent his son Trong Thuy to sign the peace accord, with the real mission of discovering the secret of Au Lac's invincibility.

Accompanied by a retinue of servants and a multitude of gifts, the young prince presented himself to King An Duong Vuong, explaining that, as a sign of goodwill, his father had appointed him to establish a new friendship between their two countries. Desiring to show himself willing to compromise, An Duong Vuong admitted the young man to his court at once. In the final reckoning, Trong Thuy was endowed with both seductive good manners and a quick mind. He soon became firm friends with the ruler's beloved daughter, Princess My Chau, "the softness of pearl." For her part, the young lady's singular beauty made a great impression on Trong Thuy—as all the court poets sang, she had "the eyebrows of a moth and the eyes of a phoenix." The young persons soon developed tender feelings for each other. Pleased by the company of Trong Thuy and favorably regarding an alliance that would seem to seal the peaceful coexistence of the two kingdoms, An Duong Vuong unhesitatingly gave him My Chau's hand in marriage.

Time passed, the prince felt an ever-growing love for his wife, who had the freshness and the innocence of a newly opened flower. But in spite of this, he never forgot that his father had sent him to Au Lac for a specific purpose. One day when he was walking with My Chau in the courtyard, he assumed a worried expression, sighed, fidgeted, showed his displeasure in a thousand ways, until his wife finally asked him what was troubling him. Had someone or something displeased him?

"It is nothing," he replied. "It is just that I still feel like a stranger in Au Lac despite our marriage and the alliance between our two kingdoms. Even though I have the honor of being your husband, I have never seen the weapon that is the source of your father's power."

"If that is all it requires to sooth your bad temper, I can easily put you at your ease," My Chau said with a smile. Wanting to prove her love to Trong Thuy and her trust in him, she took him to the highest tower in the citadel and showed him the crossbow.

In response to his cunning questions, she immediately told him the story of the golden tortoise's gift. The prince listened attentively, carefully noting each detail of the event. He secretly had a copy made of the claw and organized for it to be set into the crossbow in place of the real one. Then he petitioned the king. "I will soon have been in Au Lac for a year, and I have been very happy during this time.

However, my marriage should not make me forget my filial duties. I wish, if you will allow me, to return to my father for a while and pay him my respect. I will come back again quickly." An Duong Vuong listened to him good-heartedly and gave his consent with a nod of his head.

The time came for the two lovers to separate. Trong Thuy genuinely felt severe regret at the idea of betraying the king, who had received him so warmly, and My Chau, who had loved him so blindly. But his loyalty to his father remained stronger than either of these emotions. He was unable to hide the sorrow in his eyes and voice when he said goodbye to My Chau. She was alarmed but did not dare to interrupt him when he made this simple declaration: "My dear wife, no one knows what the future might bring. We know about the feelings that unite us but we cannot be as sure about the fragile political alliance that binds our two nations. Who knows what might become of us?" Aware that his sorrow was too severe for a brief and simple separation, she sensed that some danger was at hand.

"If, for some reason or another, I am forced to leave the City of the Conch," she told him, "I will take the gold brocade cloak lined with goose feathers that you gave me. I will drop a feather at each crossroad so that you can follow my trail." Without giving Trong Thuy time to reply, she briefly bowed her face to hide her tears, and retired to her apartments.

Several weeks passed. The prince met no obstacles and soon reached his father's kingdom. He gave Trieu Da the precious claw and the emperor immediately sent his troops to attack Au Lac. When the news reached An Duong Vuong, the king was busy playing chess. Almost completely unmoved, he said in a cold voice, "The general is out of his mind! Has he forgotten my crossbow?" The king did not even bother to interrupt the game and waited until the Chinese army was at the gates of the citadel before going to fetch his supernatural weapon. At the first shot, he realized the deception. Trieu Da's warriors had begun to scale the walls, and they ran through the entire city without encountering any resistance, massacring the inhabitants each step of the way as they advanced. An Duong Vuong had barely enough time to go and find My Chau, who had sought refuge in her quarters. He immediately took her by the hand and they leapt onto a horse.

The king left the town, which was engulfed in blood and fire, spurring his mount forward as best he could in the hope of escaping his pursuers. As he did so, My Chau wept and pressed herself against her father while pulling off handfuls of goose feathers to drop at each crossroads, indicating the direction they had taken. No matter how excellent a horseman the king was, the hours passed, days passed, they galloped, they galloped, they galloped, and the enemy always followed close behind them. When they reached the sea, the king heard a squad of men approaching and he realized that he was lost. "Heaven has abandoned me!" he cried. "Ambassador of the Tranquil Waters, wherever you are, please help me!"

The golden tortoise appeared, floating on the sea. "O king, how can you escape the enemy you carry behind yourself?" An Duong

Vuong turned around and pulled his daughter closer to him to protect her. But instead of a fierce foe, he could see only his beloved daughter. Was it possible? He looked at her as though she were a stranger.

Her eyes reddened as she wept. Prostrating herself, My Chau said, "Father, forgive me, I beg you. A certain person abused my trust and my innocence. I never wanted to betray you or my country." Without saying a word, the king struck the young girl with his sword, and she died with a single blow. Then he climbed down from his horse and walked into the path through the waters that the golden tortoise had opened before him. He was never heard of again.

When Trong Thuy and his army reached the beach, they found no trace of An Duong Vuong. On the other hand, he was deeply distressed to discover the motionless body of My Chau, whose blood had run into the sea in all directions. He threw himself on her and for a long time held his wife tightly, she who had been sacrificed on the altar of filial duty. Although his father encouraged him to participate in the victory celebrations the following night before enjoying himself as he pleased, he could do nothing. He wandered along the corridors of the palace where he and his dearly beloved had been so happy, and finally threw himself into the pond where she loved to bathe, and drowned.

Since that day, the legends say, the oysters of the beach where the princess lost her life produce precious rose-colored pearls. If one washes them in the water where Trong Thuy died, they take on, so it is said, an incomparable fragrance.

9

The Woman Who Waited

There was once a young man who lived in a village in the High Region together with his sister, who was barely six years old. They had lost both their parents in a flood during the rainy season. Alone in the world from that time on, they lived completely for each other. He tenderly protected her, and she brightened his life with her laughter, her happiness, and the songs she sang to make the time pass more quickly. Their house was extremely poor and their life was difficult, but it was enough for them to look at each other to forget their precarious existence.

One morning the little girl suggested to her brother that they should go to the spring festival, which the whole village was preparing to celebrate. The young man followed her. They strolled through the festivities, the lively conversations, the smell of incense, roasted meats, and steamed buns, past men and women dressed in long embroidered blouses and satin trousers, garments that saw the light only once a year. The two stopped in front of an old man who offered to tell their fortune. The girl pushed her brother forward. He accepted, smiling.

The man looked at them tentatively and asked their dates of birth before making several quick calculations on a piece of paper. After several minutes of silence he said, "If these really are the hour and day of your births, you are destined to marry your sister. Nothing can alter the course of your fate." The prediction frightened the orphans. But if the young girl quickly forgot his words, the young man was never able to let go of them. The idea haunted him night and day, giving him no respite. He hid his worries as best he could but he was never able to chase the old man's words out of his mind.

He made a desperate decision. One day when he was going into the forest to cut wood, he invited his sister to come with him. They went farther into the forest than they had ever been before but she followed him without any fear, apparently trusting him completely. The sun passed over the interwoven leaves and the air hummed with the songs of birds. She bent over to pick a wild orchid. The young man raised his axe and brought it down on the nape of the child's neck before running away. He walked day after day, pursued by his crime and haunted by the image of his silent sister sprawled out silently on the ground.

He was still not freed from his major obsession. He decided to change his name and to change the details of his past life. He settled several hundred kilometers away, at Long Son. Gradually, time quieted his guilt and he found peace once more. Innumerable years rolled by, and having no more than a bare subsistence to maintain, the young man began to take risks. He became a successful cloth merchant and an established businessman. Soon he married a daughter of one of his merchant friends. She was beautiful and considerate, and brought him much joy. He loved to watch her coming and going about the house, arranging the curtains, straightening up a flower in a vase. He loved her long black hair that covered her back like a tightly woven veil. And he contentedly imagined himself growing old by her side.

The birth of a handsome and intelligent son added a final touch to his happiness. However, the happiness of this fine, virtuous young man was completely overturned one day when he entered the inner courtyard of their home and found his wife sitting in the sunlight, busy drying her hair after she had just washed it. She had her back turned to him and did not notice his arrival. Just as she lifted her long hair to slide an ebony comb through it, he noticed a scar, a thick white line under the nape of the young woman's neck.

Frightened, he asked his companion about the origin of the wound. After a few seconds of silence, she lowered her eyes and told her story. "I am actually only the adopted daughter of the man I call my father. In reality, I am an orphan. When I was a child, I lived with my brother, who meant everything to me. We were poor but we were happy because we were so attached to each other. Almost twenty years ago we went into a forest and he hit me with his axe, leaving this scar. He ran away, abandoning me. I was rescued by a band of robbers. But they were forced to leave their den in order to escape from the guardians, who then discovered me. A passing merchant who had lost his daughter had pity on me and adopted me. I don't know what became of my brother and I have never been able to explain his actions. We loved each other very much."

The woman cried as the man insisted on finding out the name of her real father and that of the village where she was born. When all his doubts had been addressed, he struggled to control his emotions. But although he had the strength not to reveal anything himself, shame and horror stopped him from looking at her or speaking at all from then on, even though he continued to love her. Soon it became impossible to live together and he left on the pretext of traveling to engage in some business.

During the first six months of his absence, his wife waited patiently. But after more than a year had passed, she was still alone without any news of him. Each day it became her habit to climb a nearby mountain with her baby in her arms, to find some higher point from which she could watch for her husband's return. Once she reached the summit, she always remained there for many hours, her eyes fixed on the horizon, hoping to see the sail of her beloved's ship come into view.

A little before the village, to the right of the road that goes to the High Region, there is a small isolated mountain with a tall rock at its very peak. Some travelers decided to stop there overnight, in the middle of nowhere, as they followed the road that snaked its long way through the mountains. Having walked since early morning, they arrived there at the end of the day and were amazed to see that the setting sun shone on the rock in such a way that it strangely resembled a woman holding a child, a woman with her back turned to them, staring down towards the river, towards the forest, towards the bright light as it slowly died. A woman in silhouette against the sky, unmoving as she waits through all eternity.

10

The Lake of the Returned Sword

Many centuries ago the Chinese ruled Vietnam. The Ming dynasty displayed great power, together with great injustice and intolerance. The people suffered terribly. While imports diminished, need and poverty continually increased. Oppression prevailed everywhere. Floods destroyed crops and aroused the starving population. An uprising took place in Thanh Hoa Province under the leadership of one man, Le Loi. But although the rebels fought with great courage, they went from one defeat to another. Fighting against troops that had superior numbers, held better weapons, and were better fed, they were forced to retreat to a mountain covered with bamboo bushes.

The emperor of the seas, Lac Long Quan, took pity on the enslaved nation and decided to intervene. At that time, there was a fisherman living in Thanh Hoa Province called Kim Minh. Each morning he got into his boat and sailed out to the open waters to cast his net. One fine day when he was fishing, he felt something that was so heavy it almost broke the mesh of his net. "With a little bit of luck, I might have caught the biggest fish that Thanh Hoa has ever seen!" he thought, delighted by his good fortune. But to his great disappointment, instead of the miraculous fish he had hoped for, there was nothing but an iron bar, which he threw back into the sea. He moved away several dozen meters, cast his net again, waited, and caught the iron bar a second time. He swore, then threw the useless piece of metal away again. Then he repeated his previous actions with the same result. Anger gave way to astonishment, and Kim Minh examined his catch more closely. "This is the blade of a sword!" he cried. It simply lacked a hilt. And even without its handle, he could see that it was a superior weapon.

Taking a thousand precautions, he brought the precious object to his hut and placed it in a box near his bed. Some time passed. The fisherman joined the rebels and fought against the oppressors. One night later on he received Le Loi and his lieutenants as guests when they were searching for a safe place to rest. Exhausted by their journey, they sat near the fire, warming their weary limbs. Once his eyes had grown accustomed to the darkness of the cabin, Le Loi noticed something shining through the spaces between the slats of a large wooden box. He approached the chest and discovered the blade of a sword. "What is that doing here? And where is the hilt? With the hilt, it would be a worthy weapon for the emperor himself!"

He then turned to Kim Minh, who told him the story of how he had cast his net three times . . .

After they had drunk a little green tea and restored their strength, the soldiers resumed their march and Le Loi himself quickly forgot the strange story that his host had told him. There were further battles but the rebels continued to experience defeat after defeat. Weeks passed, then months, and their morale became lower and lower. One day, after they had beaten a retreat yet again, Le Loi and his soldiers withdrew to the forest. While they were riding, Le Loi suddenly saw a bright light at the top of a banyan tree. He rode straight towards the banyan, then dismounted and climbed the tree. The light came from a sword hilt engraved with gold and covered with jade. The hilt shone like a thousand mirrors under the midday sun.

Dazzled, Le Loi concentrated so that he could examine the object more closely. "It is strange. I have never seen this hilt before, but it seems familiar." Then Kim Minh's story came back to him. He immediately leapt onto his mount and rode to the fisherman's hut, followed by his faithful troops. The blade fitted the hilt perfectly.

"My lord," Kim Minh stated, "there can be no doubt that this is a gift to you from heaven. The weapon is of divine origin. It is a sign that your quest is just." Raising the sacred sword, Le Loi inspired his followers. From that day on, he was continually victorious against the Ming. Soon the whole country was freed from the Chinese yoke and Le Loi was crowned king.

A year passed. Le Loi had established peace and ruled the country wisely. His subjects showed him a respect and admiration that bordered on veneration. The new sovereign remained humble and spent all his leisure hours sailing on Ta Vong Lake in the middle of the capital. One fine day, the path of his boat was blocked by an immense golden tortoise that burst up from the depths of the lake. She spoke to Le Loi in a human voice. "O king, you have made good use of the present my master gave you. Now that the invaders have been driven out, and order and prosperity have returned, you no longer need our aid."

Le Loi felt the sword quiver at these words, as if it were impatient to return to the place from where it had come. Understanding that he had benefited from the protection of Lac Long Quan, he bowed to the messenger, took the weapon from its sheath and threw it towards the tortoise, which opened its mouth and caught the weapon with a single leap, before diving down into the lake and disappearing. Standing on his boat decorated with dragons and golden brown phoenixes, the king contemplated for a long time the waters that had closed around the tortoise, like a thick veil. Today this lake, which is situated in the middle of Hanoi, is known as the Lake of the Returned Sword.

11

The Miraculous Pearl

There was once a hunter named Da Trang. He lived alone in a shack and was content to have very little, bartering the game he caught for rice, clothing, and the most basic necessities. At the bottom of his garden, which contained the ruins of an old temple, lived two shining black serpents that were unusually beautiful. At first he had been a bit afraid of them. Then, seeing that they left him in peace, he grew accustomed to their presence, so much so that he often left them pieces of meat when he had some to spare.

One day, he heard a savage hissing and he rushed to the end of the garden, where he saw an enormous yellow serpent attacking the two black snakes. He took his bow and fired it. The arrow hit the aggressor and he fled. But one of the black snakes had been mortally wounded. Da Trang sadly buried it behind the temple. That night, an old man dressed in a splendid robe of jet black embroidered silk appeared to him in a dream.

"You have saved me from my enemy the yellow cobra, and you have given my companion a proper grave. In recognition of my gratitude, I would like to give you a gift." He drew a phosphorescent pearl out from the sleeve of his gown. It was as big as the man's thumbnail. "Place it under your tongue and you will be able to understand what the animals are saying, whether they have scales, feathers, or fur. No beast will be able to hide its secrets from you."

When Da Trang awoke at dawn, he saw the pearl right next to his pillow. He put it in his mouth before he set out to go hunting. When he reached the edge of the forest, he heard a voice calling out to him. "I know how to find antelope, hind and roe deer, hare and wild boar, fowls and jungle roosters. All you have to do is to listen to me. You won't regret it!"

Da Trang raised his head and realized who was talking: a crow was staring intensely at him. "And what do you want for your troubles?" The bird obviously understood him. "Just leave me the entrails, nothing but the entrails," he cried out before flying away, pointing out a thicket to Da Trang.

The hunter found a wild boar hiding there and, as they had agreed, left the innards at the foot of the bush. From then on, the man and the bird became partners, Da Trang always making sure that the crow had his share of the booty. But one day some animal or other stole the entrails that were meant for the crow before the bird had returned from the forest. On finding nothing waiting for him, the bird assumed that Da Trang had forgotten him. Flying to the man, the bird demanded his due. The hunter did his best to explain, but his partner refused to believe him. The discussion turned into a dispute and Da Trang was forced to draw his bow to drive the crow away. He fired one arrow that missed the bird. The bird seized the arrow and flew away helter-skelter, holding it in his claws.

Less than a week passed before the hunter was arrested by the local authorities. An arrow had been discovered bearing his name, its tip stuck deep down the throat of a drowned man. It was useless to protest his innocence. No one believed him, and whether he liked it or not, he was forced to spend time in prison. At first, the wardens were of the opinion that he had lost his mind. He talked to himself in his cell and he laughed at jokes that no one else there could hear. In fact, Da Trang was quite simply talking with the bugs, mosquitoes, and mice that populated the prison, begging some of them not to sting him and others to bring him news from the outside world, making a thousand efforts not to crush any of his tiny companions who conversed good-heartedly with him.

One morning when he was questioning a row of ants that were slowly moving their reserves up the wall, he learned that a flood, such as had not been seen in the country for a decade, was on its way. Beating his metal mug against the bars of his cell, he called the guards and asked to see the director of the prison, announcing that he had vital information to give him. At first incredulous, the head of the prison was eventually persuaded because Da Trang himself seemed so convinced by what he was saying. Besides, he had seen that this prisoner often had surprising intuitions that never failed to come true. So he went to speak to the governor of the province, who took appropriate steps and, as a precautionary measure, ordered people who lived near the river to evacuate their homes. A few days later, exactly as had been predicted, a terrible flood submerged the fields to a depth of several hundred meters, destroying the fields and the rice crops. The governor immediately implemented an emergency plan. Da Trang was henceforth treated more considerately and the conditions of his existence were much improved. He seemed to be some sort of oracle.

Some time later, he overheard a conversation between some sparrows that had set up a clay nest on a wall to store grain.

"Hurry up! Hurry up!" one of them exclaimed. "We only have a few days to gather plenty of food."

"But where does all this rice come from?" the other bird asked.

"From a load of grain organized by a king from the north," replied the first sparrow. "He intends to make a surprise attack on this country, and in order to support his troops in the forthcoming battles, he has prepared large amounts of food for his soldiers. However, one of his carts fell into a ravine and this has slowed them down. He has to wait for the next delivery so as to have enough supplies, and that won't come for another week! While they are waiting, we have a wonderful opportunity to take his grain. So, hurry up, I beseech you, before the others have wind of this!"

On hearing these words, Da Trang immediately asked for permission to speak to the king. The governor, who now had complete faith in him, arranged an interview with his majesty. Da Trang, his head bowed, told the ruler what he had heard. The necessary steps were taken at once, and the enemy, who had expected to benefit from a surprise attack, suffered the very opposite of what they had hoped for—a terrible defeat that almost annihilated them all. The invading troops were pushed back beyond the frontiers of the state, and for several whole days the country feasted in celebration of this extraordinary victory.

Da Trang received the status of a minister and the king treated him with an embarrassing familiarity. In response to his questions, the king learned Da Trang's whole history, from the serpents at the temple to the deviousness of the crow. Da Trang did not hesitate to show the king the pearl, which shone like the sun.

The king was a just man. Although he could see the immense possibilities that were open to him by being able to understand the languages of all the animals, he did not want to deprive his friend of the gift he had received. He simply decided to keep Da Trang close by so that he could have any potentially interesting conversations translated straightaway.

Thus Da Trang began a new and happy stage of his life, living near the king, telling him about the conversations between the insects, rodents, birds, but also the horses, elephants, and wild cats. They traveled throughout the entire kingdom and were able, in this way, to learn the mores and customs that shaped the beasts' societies, their hierarchies, their rules, and their needs. They soon realized that animals are basically not very different from humans. There are good ones and bad, brave ones and cowards, wise ones and fools. Some are weak and others are strong, and malice sometimes suffices to change who is brave and who is weak. Justice and injustice are distributed just as equally over the realms of the animals as they are among human beings.

After land came the sea. The king's curiosity was insatiable and Da Trang was even more disposed to humoring him. The whole court set out in ships and junks to listen to the chattering of the shrimps and the crustaceans, the shellfish, the large and small fish. After a while, however, people began to grow weary of these conversations. If humans are wrong to misunderstand animals, it is true that beasts do have their faults and their petty ways of behaving, such that a conversation between a tortoise and a seagull can be no more interesting than that of two gossips in a marketplace.

The king therefore gave the order, one beautiful spring morning, to start back home. It was time to return to the palace and to take an interest in some of the things that were happening in that world. While the ships were retracing their path, Da Trang was sitting on the deck in the sun, when he suddenly heard a humming noise. Bending down beneath the ship's rail, he saw a charming little cuttlefish swimming through the water near the royal vessel and singing as it swam:

Cloud, white cloud,

Swimming, slowly swimming

Through the blue waters of the sky . . .

The spectacle of this charming cuttlefish singing in time with its movement through the water was truly irresistible. Da Trang burst out laughing and almost choked on the pearl. He coughed, and despite his best efforts, it fell into the sea. His joy ceased at once and, desperate, he called for the best divers on board to recover his treasure. They dived down again and again, determinedly searching beneath the large restless waves. It was all in vain. Despite Da Trang's pleas and tears, everyone was forced to admit in the end that it was an impossible enterprise.

The king expressed his regret over and over again, but his sorrow was nothing compared to Da Trang's immense grief. Nothing could cheer him up, and all the favors of the king, who remembered all the pleasure and instruction Da Trang had given him, failed to console him. Day and night he wandered about thinking of the vanished pearl, until eventually a crazy idea germinated in his exhausted brain. He would gather hundreds of energetic people and set them to pouring one cartload of sand after another into the ocean, in order to fill up the sea, as if his pearl might somehow come to the surface in this way. At first the king allowed Da Trang to do this in the hope that he would see the futility of such endeavors and regain his senses. But faced with such extraordinary obstinacy, the king eventually had no choice but to stop these efforts and forbid his poor friend from approaching the shore. Obsessed with the pearl, his mind destroyed and his body weakened, the despondent Da Trang soon died. His last wish was to be buried at the spot where he had witnessed the progress of these impossible efforts, facing the sea that had swallowed his treasure forever.

For all that, his unsatisfied soul was never able to leave the world of the living. It is told that he was reincarnated in small Da Trang crabs. You often come across them at the beach at low tide. They spend all their time rolling little balls of sand along the ground with their claws. It only needs one tiny wave to dissolve the balls, but far from being discouraged, they resume their activities once more as if nothing had happened, rolling the sand into balls again and again until a new wave sweeps them away. And on it goes, again and again, in an endless cycle.

12

Gold and Starfruits

There were once two brothers who were as different in appearance as they were in character. The older brother, who was as ugly as could be, was abundantly endowed with a heart of stone and a mind most black. Being of a naturally lazy disposition, he loved nothing more than to lounge around the family house, leaving his younger brother to undertake all the chores and work in the fields. The latter, who was remarkably handsome, had no equal with regard to his kindness and generosity. He helped anyone who needed his assistance, sparing no effort to do so, and always treated his neighbors with great respect. The difference between these two men of the same blood never failed to attract numerous comments from members of the village where they lived. These rumors always exasperated the older brother, who would have loved to have been praised the way his brother was, though he was unwilling to make any effort to deserve such honors. That goes without saying.

When their parents died, they left the sons a large inheritance—a beautiful house, large enough for several families, and an orchard; fertile rice fields; livestock, including oxen, goats and pigs; and a stony small field, with a beautiful starfruit tree. The years passed and the brothers decided to marry. As was appropriate, they chose women exactly like themselves. The older brother's wife was also selfish, vain, and greedy. The younger brother's wife, on the other hand, was as patient as she was prudent, hard working, and modest as well—a real pearl.

After the weddings had been celebrated, the older brother called the younger brother and said, "Can you see that now that we are married, I think it would be best if we each pursued our own lives in our own ways. As I am the oldest, I should bear the costs for looking after the family altar and the worship of the ancestors, and these are very heavy. I won't be able to do that unless I keep the house, the orchard, the rice fields, and the livestock."

"And what is left for me, dear brother?" the younger brother gently asked.

"Well, the field to the east, to be sure, and the starfruit tree! I seem to remember that there is a small straw hut too, where you can live from now on. It's a perfect place to begin family life. For two strong and virtuous young people like yourselves, it should be quite sufficient," he added in a cynical tone.

The younger brother knew that the family house was large enough to accommodate his wife and himself, but he did not utter a single word. In accordance with Confucian precepts, he was bound to obey and respect his older brother. He asked his wife to help him pack their meager belongings before they went to settle in the small hut near the starfruit tree. The older brother watched mockingly as the couple took possession of the small parcel of land they had been given without any display of discontent or regret. They reinforced the walls of their new lodgings and painted them white. They set about cultivating the stony field that they knew would never yield enough to repay them for their efforts. "For the moment, this is all we need. We are young and resilient and we can work hard. Surely we can find employment with people who are rich."

"Unless we fall sick or have children," his wife observed, "we shouldn't have any problems."

By chance, they had inherited the starfruit tree. A magnificent tree that they carefully looked after, it gave them sweet, bright yellow, juicy fruit, which they sold at the market, while keeping some small amount for their more difficult days. They diligently watered the roots of the tree, killed the parasites, and guarded the ever increasing number of fruit, waiting for them to ripen. Each morning as he set out for the fields, each evening when he returned home, the younger brother paused to contemplate his tiny treasure, his heart full of pride for this tree that was almost collapsing under the weight of the starfruits.

One evening, he startled a bird with fiery golden plumage that was sitting at the top of the tree, happily eating the almost ripe fruits. For a moment he thought of chasing the bird away in order to preserve his precious crop, but then he changed his mind. "Two or three pieces won't make any difference," he told himself. "And the bird is so beautiful . . ." Trying to be very quiet, he went to find his wife, so that she too could come and admire the extraordinary animal. The scarlet top of the bird's head was speckled with gold spots, like a crown, and, in the setting sunlight, its slim body seemed to be covered with thousands of precious stones. The woman's heart broke as she stared at the bird for a long time.

"Oh bird, beautiful bird, please don't peck all our fruit," she murmured. "It is all we have and our only hope of survival."

To her great amazement, she saw the bird turn towards her and speak in a human voice. "Don't be afraid," it said. "For each fruit I eat, I will give you a nugget of gold, as big as your own generous hearts. I am not one of those creatures who take but give nothing in return. Make a sack three spans wide, no larger. And when your husband comes to find me tomorrow at this same hour, he will not be sorry." With these words, the bird flew away in a whirlwind of fire, not even bothering to say goodbye to the astonished couple.

The husband and wife looked at each other in disbelief. Had they been dreaming? Taking a chance, the wife made a bag in the dimensions the bird had given to her husband, who then waited at the appointed time near the starfruit tree. At the precise moment, the bird kept its rendezvous. It gracefully landed on the ground and, bending down, invited the man to climb up on its back. "You'll see,

we'll be there in no time at all!" And they took flight as if the younger
brother weighed no more than a feather. They flew over magnificent
landscapes: deserts white as salt, dark green forests, crystal waterfalls,
azure oceans sparkling in the scattered rays of the sun. The man did
not say a word. He was struck dumb by the spectacle that unfolded
before his eyes. There were so many marvelous things he had never
known about!

But they were nothing compared to what awaited him. After
several hours, the bird turned towards an isolated mountain. It
landed on a sort of small plateau, and pointing out a hidden entrance,
indicated to the man that he should enter, picking up a large jewel
with its claw as it did so. "You will find more riches here than you
have ever seen before. Fill your sack but don't take any more than
that. And you will have enough for you and your wife for many
generations to come."

The younger brother restrained a gasp as he entered the grotto.
The whole ground was covered with nothing but shining nuggets:
sapphires blue as the night, rubies that seemed to be filled with fire,
pearls as big as a man's fist, and rows of diamonds that looked like
rivers. All the colors of the rainbow were here, all the shapes—round,
rectangular, octagonal—and all possible sizes. Together they shone
like a thousand fires, almost blinding the man unless he covered
his eyes.

He could hardly tear himself away from the marvelous vision.
Then, remembering that the spirit bird was waiting for him, he began

filling his sack with gold. After hesitating a few times, he added a pearl and a ruby. He passed one last look over the fabulous treasures in the cavern, then went outside to rejoin his companion. The bird glanced at the sack and exclaimed, "But you haven't even filled your sack yet! Go back inside the cave. There is still plenty of time."

The man politely declined the offer. "I have enough to live comfortably. I don't need any more. With this gold, we can buy a house worthy of the name, some land, and one or two oxen to work it. My wife is well provided for. I will have this pearl mounted in a pendant. As for this ruby, we will keep it in memory of you and your kindness. It is exactly the same color as your feathers." Nothing the bird could say would change his mind. So it offered a position on its back to the younger brother once more and they left.

The faithful wife watched the part of the sky where her husband had disappeared on his celestial vehicle. She was greatly relieved to see a black dot emerge, which slowly grew larger and larger. The man she loved was coming back. From anxiety she soon passed to the pinnacle of joy when he showed her the gold and precious stones he had brought. The material cares that had previously overwhelmed them were now no more than a bad memory, and the pair turned towards their benefactor and thanked it profusely. The bird bowed its head, wished them long and happy lives, and then, with a flap of its wings, took to the azure sky.

After that, being richer than any of the notables in the region, the couple built a new home and bought wet, fertile rice fields that produced abundant grain. Everything smiled on them. Abundance and harmony seemed to be the keywords of their new existence. They remained humble and hard-working, never hesitating to put their hands into their purses when those less fortunate than themselves were in need. The village continually rang with their great praise, to the immense displeasure of the elder brother, who promised himself that he would find out the secret behind this sudden prosperity.

Taking advantage of his younger brother's respectful invitation to come and visit him in his new dwelling, he tried to contain himself as he questioned his host in an almost indifferent manner. As his brother told him the very smallest details of his dealings with the starfruit tree, about the sacred bird and the treasure buried inside the mountain, his heart beat with unrestrained greed. The treasure was worthy of the Jade Emperor himself. He must have it whatever the cost! But he cunningly hid his thoughts under honeyed words, even though he harbored great malice towards the brother who, in his kind-heartedness, would never have doubted him for a moment.

"Little brother, I have treated you unfairly," he said, assuming a contrite expression. "You have done badly from the division of our inheritance, and I feel very sad about that. Not a day passes when I don't think about it. So I have come to visit you today in order to make amends for my faults. I beg you to come and live in the family home, while my wife and I make do with the east field and its straw hut."

The younger brother and his wife protested vigorously that they had all they needed, but the older brother was immovable. He insisted, he said, that a proper balance should be restored, and the two listeners finally agreed with him. They did not suspect that his cunning proposal, far from being driven by some feeling of guilt, was only a way to get his hands on the precious starfruit tree.

No sooner said than done. The older brother installed himself in the wretched shack, dressed himself in rags, and waited for the return of the miraculous bird. His wish was quickly granted. One afternoon he saw the supernatural beast perch at the top of the carambola tree and peck at all the fruits he desired.

"Poor me!" the brother lamented, uttering perfectly rehearsed sobs. "I have nothing to live on but these starfruits, and look, something is stealing them! I will surely die of hunger."

The bird replied, "Don't worry. I never owe anything to anyone. Prepare yourself for tomorrow, this same place, same time, and bring a sack three handspans wide, not one span larger. You will not be deceived, I promise you." And with these words, the spirit bird flew away.

The older brother rejoiced. Those were the words he had been waiting to hear. He immediately ordered his wife to bring him a sack—but just three spans when there was more treasure at his disposal than any mortal had ever known? The bigger the better! They both agreed. Not three, not ten, not even twenty spans would be enough. So it turned out that when the older brother confidently climbed onto the spirit bird's back, he was carrying a sack almost large enough to hold them both. "I told you three handspans!" said the bird angrily.

"That's fine," the man replied. "But when you've lived your whole life in poverty, as I have, you like to take precautions, that's all." Sighing, the bird shook its head and took to the air with the older brother on its back.

The brother paid no attention to the lands they were passing over. He could only think of one thing—the beautiful treasure that would soon be his. Tightly holding onto the bird's feathers, he sorted through the items in his mind—the bars and nuggets of gold, the weight of the various-sized diamonds, the many hiding places he could build to hold the precious objects—passing the whole time with these useless calculations. Finally the mountain came into view, and as soon as the bird landed, he rushed towards the entrance to the cave. It was dazzling! Not content to stuff the immense bag he had brought with gold and jewels, he also joined the tails of his jacket and filled them with emeralds, tied his trouser legs together and stuffed them with pearls, and hid diamonds and rubies in each pocket of his vest. And so, staggering under the weight of all he had gathered, he returned to the entrance of the cave.

He perched as comfortably as he could on the back of the bird and refused to listen when the creature told him that he was much too heavy for the trip back. "Don't pretend to be so stingy," he sniggered. "I've only taken what I need. This should satisfy the owners of the starfruit tree for many years more." When the bird realized that any comment it made would only slide off him like water off a rock, it groaned and rose into the air with considerable difficulty. Normally lighter than air, it swayed with great difficulty to hold its course. And it had not yet covered a thousand *truong* before it felt it was becoming weaker. "Throw away some of your gold," it cried to the man. "I can't carry it all."

"What did you say?" he replied. "Throw away my gold? Are you mad?" And he held his sack against him more tightly than ever. However, he was also afraid because he could see that instead of flying high above the ocean as they did when they came to the island, they were now flying dangerously close to it. But his fear was not as strong as his greed.

"Lighten my load if you don't want to die," the bird called out one last time. But the man, despite these pleas, desperately clung to his gold. Nothing in the world could make him let go of it, even when the golden brown wings of the bird skimmed just above the waves. Exhausted, the bird dropped onto the ocean. The older brother was shocked and rolled off its back, falling into the water with a loud "plop." Relieved of its burden, the fabulous creature quickly regained altitude. As for the man, while debating how he could rise to the surface and live, he well and truly ended up losing the sack anyway. But it was too late—the weight of the other valuables he had stored in every part of his clothing dragged him down to the bottom of the ocean, and he disappeared forever, taking his useless treasure with him.

13

The Lake Born in One Night

There was once a princess who bore the lovely name Tien Dung, which means "as beautiful as a fairy." She had large dark eyes, a complexion of smooth pearl, and her features were so fine that people thought a kind and beautiful fairy must have landed on her cradle and shaped her delicate face. Many princes from neighboring countries asked for her hand in marriage. But unlike most young women, be they beautiful or ugly, be they the daughters of peasants or of mandarins, Tien Dung had no desire to be married. The years passed and no one could find the path to her heart. She seemed to love only one thing: sailing about and endlessly discovering new places. Each spring, she asked for her father's permission to sail along the beautiful lands of Van Lang, and she never returned until it was time for the birds to migrate back from the north. The king, incapable of refusing her smallest request, gave her an elegant boat decorated with dragons and phoenixes, and a large troop of soldiers to protect and serve her whatever the circumstances. He hoped that one day she would change her mind and marry a prince from a neighboring country, which would create a useful strategic alliance for his kingdom. At the same time, he was happy to have his favorite daughter close by his side.

One day, the vessel carrying the princess and her retinue arrived at a charming village. The picturesque site pleased Tien Dung and she decided to stop there so she could explore the area. She walked along the beach and, finding it to be very clean, decided to take advantage of the wonderful climate and the beauty of the spot by ordering a bathing shelter to be erected. The servants prepared an impromptu tent from some lengths of silk and the princess began to bathe. While she was splashing water on her back, she heard a soft cry. Turning around, she found herself almost nose to nose with a young man who was entirely naked. He had tried in vain to hide behind the clump of reeds and she had accidently splashed him. Seized with fear, she almost called her attendants to help her, but she was amused by the young man's confusion, and for all that, he was quite handsome. Half buried in the sand, he did not dare raise his eyes to look at Tien Dung and implored her forgiveness as he told her about his life.

"Princess, my name is Chu Dong Tu. I used to live with my father in a shack on the bank of a river. We were poor but we never complained. We had a roof over our heads and the sea always provided us with enough to eat. But one day when we were out fishing, a fire destroyed our cabin and the few possessions we owned. It was a terrible blow, and we were reduced to such poverty in the end that we finally only had one cotton loincloth between the two of us. We took it in turns to wear the cloth when we went to the market to sell our fish. Having no clothes worthy of the name to protect us from the cold, my father fell gravely ill. He was old and not strong like I am. He died in a few weeks. He wanted me to have the cloth, arguing that he would have no need of it where he was going, but I didn't have the heart to obey him. He deserved a decent burial and I wrapped his remains in the only piece of material I had at my disposal.

"Since then, I spend almost all my time submerged in water, selling fish, crabs, and shellfish to passing boats. I wait until the shores are deserted so that I can return to a nearby tiny straw hut where I live, and when night falls, I go out fishing when no one can see me. I have lived like that for two years now and I have still not been able to earn enough to buy a loincloth. The coming of your boat was suddenly announced by the sound of drums, gongs, and flutes, and when it arrived with flags and banners floating in the breeze, I had just enough time to hide behind these reeds. But, alas, you decided to set up your shelter at exactly this spot."

Profoundly moved by the young man's words, Tien Dung then took up the conversation. "Your filial piety does you great honor. There is nothing to be ashamed of in what you did to provide your father with a decent burial. For my part, I consider our meeting to be a sign from heaven. It is time that I was married and you will be my husband." To the great astonishment of her servants, the princess emerged from her silk enclosure accompanied by a very handsome young man covered with the simplest garb. She presented him with richly embroidered garments and ordered her servants to prepare a feast. And when Chu Dong Tu, who was both bewildered and filled with wonder at the same time, offered his feeble objections she waved them away, insisting, "Heaven has brought us together. This is our destiny. We must obey it." And their marriage was celebrated that very night on the boat.

On hearing this incredible news, the king was violently angry. "How could my daughter lower herself to associate with the first pauper she meets? She has no respect for her status or for her father. This is an unforgivable insult that deserves no mercy. If she ever dares show herself again in my presence, I will cut off her head!" Exiled forever from the palace and the court, Tien Dung and Chu Dong Tu decided to settle in the village where they had met. They threw themselves into trading so that they could live, and quickly prospered. One of the busiest markets in the region was soon established on the bank of the river and their wealth quickly increased.

One day, a foreign dealer offered to join with them in business. Overseas, he assured them, their merchandise would be worth five times more, perhaps ten times more! Tien Dung and her husband discussed the proposal. She convinced him that they should become partners with the foreign dealer. "There is no risk in it," she observed. "Heaven has sent him to us. It has watched over us and given us a comfortable living. Today there can be no doubt that it has manifested itself again."

Chu Dong Tu accompanied the trader. Their boat sailed around the southern cape and a week later entered a river that brought them to an island. Perched on a small mountain at the center of the island was a pagoda. Chu Dong Tu, wanting to stretch his legs, took a walk and came to the doors of the temple. He met a monk named Phat Quang, "the light of Buddha," who smiled as he welcomed him. "I have been waiting for you a long time, Chu Dong Tu." The monk revealed that he had been given the mission of teaching the merchant all he knew.

Chu Dong Tu decided to quit the boat, entrusting his traveling companion with the management of their joint affairs. Then he became a diligent disciple of Phat Quang, who taught him for a whole year. At the end of it the boat returned to pick up Chu Dong Tu again as they had previously agreed. When Chu Dong Tu took leave of his master, Phat Quang gave him a conical hat and a wand, telling him to keep them by his side all the time.

Business had been extremely profitable but Chu Dong Tu was completely indifferent to the gold bars they had accumulated. Material wealth was the last thing he cared about. When he returned home, he taught his wife the doctrines he had adopted. To the astonishment of the town, the couple abandoned their house, business, and goods and traveled about in search of the Way. They took nothing with them except for the monk's humble gifts.

One evening, as they were walking down a desert road and at the end of their strength, they stopped to take a little rest, planting the wand in the ground with the conical hat on top of it. Then they stretched under this precarious shelter. At the third watch, while they were still asleep, the earth trembled and shook them with great force. Opening their eyes, they were astounded to see that their makeshift resting place had changed into a precious wooden bed surrounded by silk curtains, their rags had become silken garments embroidered with gold and covered with rubies, and the walls of a palace had risen around them, the like of which they could never have imagined, encrusted with jade and mother-of-pearl. Walking out onto the balcony, they saw that the desert path they had been following until they stopped a few hours ago now led to a busy city with a marketplace, houses, and barracks. A river flowed past, full of fish, watchmen were at their posts, positioned on the surrounding walls at regular intervals, and a battalion of servants and courtiers were close at hand, ready to bring anything the astounded couple wanted.

"Where are we?" Princess Tien Dung asked.

"This is your kingdom of course, your highness," the servants respectfully replied, bowing low before her. A mandarin entered and presented them with a register describing the cumulative wealth of the kingdom: gold, silver, and precious stones, provisions, weapons, soldiers, civil and military administrators, and servants.

The news of a citadel that had been born in a single night spread like a cloud of dust, and the following day the people from the surrounding countryside surged into the capital, bringing diverse offerings to their new rulers, who assured them of their protection. The visitors found a perfectly organized city, fully outfitted with the necessary officials, together with the equipment necessary to defend the city, harvest the crops, and administer the government.

When Tien Dung's father heard this news, he was twice as angry as before. He accused his daughter of wanting to overthrow him and sent his fiercest troops to destroy the citadel. "Let the archers string their bows, let the drums play songs in praise of war. I have been betrayed and I order you to bring me the heads of this wretched couple. Succeed and I will cover you with gold and honors." Excited by his promises, the army set out. As they approached dangerously close to the city, Tien Dung's mandarins showed her a military strategy that would completely destroy the enemy. "I do not wish to oppose my father. Heaven has given us everything because I obeyed him, and I will entrust my destiny to heaven again. Let the king kill me if that is his wish. I will not raise my smallest finger in my own defense."

Night fell as the king's army reached the other side of the river across from the city. Leaving their attack until the following day, they set up camp and ordered sentries to patrol its boundaries. At dawn they placed a floating bridge across the river. The attack was only moments away when they heard a terrible rumbling. The earth shook, the pylons on the bridge tore away, trees were uprooted, terror spread among the king's soldiers, then a hurricane lifted Tien Dung's citadel into the sky. When the tempest ceased, a vast lake spread its waters across the place where the kingdom of the princess and the fisherman had once stood.

The king, realizing that he had been wrong to want to fight them, built a temple in honor of Chu Dong Tu and Tien Dung not far from the lake born in one night, which became legendary.

14
Millet Gruel

For the third time in a row, the student Lu Sinh had failed the triennial doctoral examination that qualified its graduates to serve the empire. He was very intelligent, had an excellent memory, and had worked hard so that he could recite the classics forwards and backwards, but none of it helped. He was forced to watch his comrades pass one after another, even though he knew everything there was to know. Thinking of his old parents who had placed all their hopes in him, his family who had lived in poverty for many years to give him a chance to have a career, he was filled with profound remorse.

How could he go back to his parents without the title he had so desired? How could he face the laughter when the villagers saw him return empty-handed and poor? Placing his bundle on his back, he thought sadly about these things as he walked, one step after another, feeling his heart grow heavy within him, as though it were made of stone. To add to his sorrow, rain had begun falling, and the icy drops ran down his face and back as he climbed the path through the mountains that would lead him back home. Night had come and he had scarcely gone anywhere. He was within two fingers of closing his eyes and finally ending everything. One wrong step in this rugged mountain terrain, one drop into a nearby ravine, and it would all be over forever.

Suddenly he felt a firm hand grip his shoulder. Surprised, he turned around and saw an old man dressed in a threadbare robe and wearing a serene expression on his face. It was a hermit who lived far from the world in a mountain grotto. "It is not a good idea to continue your journey at this time," he said with a smile. "Come and warm yourself by my fire. I'm cooking some millet gruel. Just rest for a little while until it is ready." Entering the cave, the student found a platform covered with a few basic cloths. He sat down and told the old man about his troubles, all that he had hoped, desired, and longed for, his plans for a career and his dreams of glory, which had now all been destroyed.

Three years later, however, Lu Sinh saw his efforts crowned with success. And what success! The first in the list of successful candidates, he heard the herald proclaim his name in a loud clear voice to an enthusiastic crowd, and he was presented at court, receiving the highest honors. Dressed in a flowing robe of a silk that was exclusively reserved for mandarins of superior rank, he was proudly paraded on a magnificent stallion through the capital, then into his own village, where his incredible success was celebrated with a wonderful feast. His parents, moved to tears, held him tightly in their arms and almost suffocated him. During the following weeks everyone looked at him with equal amounts of respect and pride, since his fame reflected on them all—neighbors, friends, and simple relatives who lived nearby and had no other claim to glory.

His rise was meteoric. Recognized by all as a first-class mind, he was equipped to undertake the highest duties in the state. Lu Sinh continually rose from one rank to another and his praises rang in everyone's mouths. He handled a number of delicate negotiations, established peace and prosperity throughout the provinces, and traveled tirelessly through the villages and countryside, creating deep and rigorous bonds that led to his further fame. In no time at all, he became the advisor the king most listened to, and he was bought to live in the court. Named first minister, he very soon married the most beautiful of the king's daughters. Their union produced exceptionally beautiful and intelligent children. Weighed down by rewards and happiness, surrounded by the most willing courtiers, confident of his good fortune, Lu Sinh enjoyed a dazzling degree of power for several years.

Then war broke out. Barbarian hordes attacked the kingdom, enslaving the population and massacring them, making no secret of their thirst for blood and terror. The emperor's army failed to drive them back. They themselves were forced to retreat, and they gave more and more territory to the invaders. Finally Lu Sinh decided to take charge of the army. The balance of forces was reversed—the enemy was repulsed and Lu Sinh's troops went from one victory to another, thanks to the way he inspired his men. He regained every village and stronghold that had been lost. When he reached the border he did not stop there, but reversing the previous situation, invaded those countries that had attempted to conquer his country. He fought their leader and cut off his head, installing himself in the city he had just won.

But, in doing this, he had exceeded the emperor's orders, and the king took offense at this disobedience. The courtiers who had once been so eager to sing Lu Sinh's praises changed their tune and talked about the possibility of him having failed. Innuendos were followed with slander, and despite the princess's entreaties, the king, who was suspicious by nature and uncomfortable at the prospect of Lu Sinh staying for so long in an enemy state, persuaded himself that his son-in-law was preparing a plot to overthrow him. With the unanimous support of his advisors, he declared Lu Sinh guilty of high treason and sent troops to bring his previous favorite back to the court as quickly as possible so that he could receive the punishment he deserved.

Caught in a surprise raid, Lu Sinh was taken prisoner. He tried to protest, to argue his innocence, and begged the emperor to listen to him, but the ruler was unshakable. Even his daughter was powerless to change his mind. Lu Sinh was thrown into prison with orders that he should be given nothing to eat or drink. He became haggard and was soon completely exhausted. His execution was to follow. The executioner made his entrance and raised his sword to cut off Lu Sinh's head. The former student closed his eyes and saw his whole life, each of the events that had led him here: his childhood poverty, his obstinate hard work, his first successes, his political triumphs, his brilliant marriage, his glorious military career, his remarkable rise followed by a fall that was equally spectacular. Then, swishing through the air, the sword came down.

Lu Sinh opened his eyes. He was in the hermit's cave, lying on a rock. A fire burned in front of him and on the fire was a small bronze pot, which his host stirred at regular intervals with a wooden spoon, tapping the side of the bowl from time to time. The rain had stopped and the old man, sensing that Lu Sinh was now awake, turned towards him with a gentle smile. "You have slept soundly for a long time. Who knows, perhaps it has given you a foretaste of the dreams of grandeur that you told me you aspire to. For my part, I have nothing but this humble fare to offer you. Nevertheless, I hope you will enjoy it."

15

The Dragon and the Immortal

Thousands and thousands of years ago, a king named Kinh Duong ruled the southern lands. Endowed with superhuman strength, he was as able to walk on water as he was to walk on land. One day when he was walking on Dong Dinh Lake, he met a beautiful princess, Long Nu, the daughter of the dragon king who ruled over the seas. The two immediately fell in love and were soon married. They gave birth to a son that had his mother's good looks and his father's physical abilities. He could snap tree trunks as easily as you might break a match, crush rocks as easily as you can break the shell of a walnut, and fall onto water the same way a cat always drops onto its paws. He was also very intelligent and shrewd. When Kinh Duong became old, he happily stepped down in favor of his son, the dragon prince, who took the throne under the name of Lac Long Quan.

At that time, the country was experiencing all sorts of difficulties and desperately needed to be united. The young king decided to begin his rule by traveling across the whole country. That was the start of such adventures as no one else, man or god, had ever known. One day while crossing the southern seas, Lac Long Quan came across some terrified villagers. A sea monster had taken residence in their region. It measured more than fifty *truong* long, swallowed human beings ten at a time, and when it swam it made waves that were higher than their houses. None of the villagers dared go to sea in their junks because the monster kept constant watch over the cave where they were sheltering. "As soon as we set out, it takes malicious pleasure in sinking our boats, then devouring the survivors. If we stay ashore, we will starve to death. Please help us, we beg you."

Lac Long Quan thought for a few minutes. "Give me a boat more solid than granite, a sword sharper than a razor, and a cauldron filled with molten metal. Then I can save you—I give you my word on that." The inhabitants of the village worked together to provide Lac Long Quan with the things for which he had asked. Armed with the sword and the cauldron, he sailed directly towards the demon fish's cavern.

While he was sailing, he shaped the molten metal into the form of a man. Lifting the object above his head, he convinced the monster that he was bringing an offering for it. He threw the metal into the air and the monster opened its mouth to swallow it with one gulp. The burning metal drove the creature mad with pain. It writhed all over and tried to sink Lac Long Quan's sturdy boat with a fierce swing of its tail. But our hero had time to leap out and, thanks to the powers he had inherited from his father, fell feet first onto the water. With one quick movement, he grabbed his sword and struck the monster, cutting it into three pieces. The battle was not over, however. The head turned into a bloodthirsty shark, a hound of the sea, whose sharp teeth almost caught the young king. Hurling chunks of earth into the river, Lac Long Quan left the shark no room to move and dealt it a fatal blow. He then threw the corpse onto a hill that has been called Cau Don Son (Dog's Head Mountain) ever since.

On returning from the river, Lac Long Quan was triumphantly carried into the village by the fishermen, who arranged a grand feast in his honor. Their gratitude was endless. Now they could go to sea without worrying about being eaten, and they could find food to feed their families.

Leaving the southern seas, Lac Long Quan sailed west. He had been told that a fox with nine tails, which was over a thousand years old, was terrorizing the land between Long Bien and Tan Vien. Each day it assumed human form and mingled with the crowds at the market in order to kidnap young girls, taking them to its den in a dark cave. None of them had ever returned. There was not a single family in the region that had not suffered from the terrible scheming of the monster. A number of men and women had even given up their homes and fields and left to find a more peaceful place in which to live.

Deeply moved by their suffering, Lac Long Quan decided to go and confront the demon in its lair. He called on the genies of the rain, the wind, and the lightning to help him, and engaged in merciless combat with the fox, whose nine tails were like tentacles, thrashing about and creating a terrifying whistling sound, ripping bushes out of the ground and throwing them at Lac Long Quan, and hurling rocks bigger than a man as if they were no more than bales of hay. They fought for three days and nights in the deafening storm, never stopping. At dawn on the fourth day, the monster, exhausted, beat a retreat. It changed into a winged serpent and tried to fly away. But, as quick as the wind, Lac Long Quan swung his sword and cut off the beast's head. Resuming its original shape, the fox's body crashed to the ground. The king retraced his path back to the lair of the beast with a few quick steps and released the prisoners. Then he ordered the powers of the land and sea to obliterate this accursed place, which had seen so many human beings suffer and die. As if by magic, the earth immediately began to shake, swallowing the cave and the mountain, and a nearby river rushed in to fill the crater that had been hollowed out. This, the largest lake in the region, was first called Fox Lake but later came to be known as the West Lake, on the edge of Hanoi.

Freed of the monster, the people rebuilt their fields and houses, and swore their allegiance to the king once more. Lac Long Quan stayed there for a while, then, seeing that the scourge was gone and peace had been reestablished, followed the road through the hills and forests to Phong Chau, where one last test was awaiting him. An old apple tree named Chien Dan grew somewhere in the forest. It was more than a thousand *truong* high. At first, its luxurious dark green leaves had been as soft as a woman's caress, but, as the years passed, they withered and dropped because a malicious demon had taken up residence in the tree and tortured everyone who passed by. It was cunning and cruel in equal portions, and continually took different shapes, using every possible disguise to trap its victims. The jungle rang with their cries and moans as it tore their bodies apart and ate them.

Lac Long Quan was more determined than ever to destroy this evil genie. He hunted it day and night, forging a path through the thick undergrowth. The sunlight could barely penetrate the thick vegetation and this made the search even more difficult. But the king was not discouraged. He examined every tree, every nook and cranny, finally finding where the demon lived.

It was the hardest fight Lac Long Quan had ever experienced. For weeks, trees and rocks flew in all directions, while clouds of ash and dust covered the world. Lac Long Quan could not overcome the evil spirit—it seemed as though the battle would never end. Finally Lac Long Quan realized that he could not defeat his opponent by the force of arms alone. He gathered all sorts of musical instruments and ordered the villagers to play them as loudly as possible. Lac Long Quan rapidly banged on an enormous brass gong. The strategy worked. The terrible cacophony frightened the demon and it fled to the other end of the earth.

To show their gratitude, the people built a large citadel in the high mountains for Lac Long Quan. However, he preferred to stay underwater in his mother's palace, in the kingdom of the seas where he had been born. He decided to live there permanently, while still promising humankind that he would come to help them in times of trouble. "If danger threatens, call me and I'll come immediately," he assured them.

Now some time later, the king of the north, De Lai, got it into his head that he would invade the beautiful southern lands. He took a mighty army with him, armed to the teeth, and was accompanied by his favorite daughter, the charming Au Co, an immortal like himself. She was so dear to him that he refused to allow her to marry any of the numerous suitors who had proposed to her. To him, none of them was worthy of her. The charms of the countryside, its exuberant and brightly colored vegetation, the richness of its wildlife, the variety of the landscape, so captivated her that she decided to stay there. Having conquered the region, De Lai had a fortified palace built for her, surrounded by a garden with alternate rows of flamboyant trees and all possible colored orchids, separated by lanes of gold and crimson. His conquest of the region met with no resistance and the people were forced to work for him from morning to night and night to morning, without any rest. But, despite the efforts of the people and their perseverance, De Lai was never satisfied, and hundreds of exhausted people died of hunger because his reign was so cruel. Eventually the inhabitants remembered Lac Long Quan's promise and together they called on him for one whole night.

In the morning, he appeared among them as if by magic and listened for a long time to their complaints about the invader—the taxes and forced labor demanded of them, their poverty, and the abuses committed by the army and by De Lai himself. Lac Long Quan assumed the form of an elegant young man and set out to find the king of the north in his citadel. But instead of the master of the realm, who was away, he met the lovely princess Au Co. Her youthfulness stunned him. She herself, contemplating the rare beauty of this stranger who was as slender as a stalk of bamboo, felt her heart almost stop beating. Overwhelmed, they looked at each other for some time, unable to say a single word. And when they could speak, all they could say was how much they loved each other. The young girl encouraged Lac Long Quan to run away with her, far from her father's tyranny. He accepted and they settled in the high mountain citadel that had previously been built in Lac Long Quan's honor.

When De Lai learned that his favorite daughter had run away with some unknown stranger, he almost exploded with rage and sent his best soldiers to pursue them, with the duty of bringing the princess back to the palace and executing the insolent wretch who had dared steal her. But this was easier said than done. With a single wave of his hand, Lac Long Quan summoned packs of wild animals to block the soldiers' path and attack them. Few of the soldiers survived the massacre, and when the savage beasts began attacking the rest of the army, De Lai was so terrified that he abandoned the south and returned to the north. Lac Long Quan had once again saved his people.

In the mountain palace, Au Co and Lac Long Quan lived in the most perfect harmony, happily enjoying every hour of every day together. Soon the princess gave birth to a small leather sack containing a hundred eggs. A week later, the eggs broke open and a hundred baby boys emerged, quickly becoming young men possessed of a strength and intelligence far beyond those of simple mortals. Years passed happily, and Lac Long Quan was troubled by only one thing: he missed the kingdom of the waters from where he had first come. One day he could bear his sorrow no longer, and changing into a dragon, he bid farewell to those he loved, telling them that he needed to return to the sea because that was where he truly belonged.

Weeks and then months passed and the lovely Au Co heard no news of Lac Long Quan. With a heavy heart, the princess climbed up the highest tower in the palace, and turning towards the southern seas, desperately cried out to the man she loved, "Oh Lac Long Quan, have you forgotten your lonely wife and children so quickly, whom you have heartlessly abandoned? Don't you know how cruel your absence and silence are to us?"

She had scarcely uttered these words when her husband, the dragon prince, appeared at her side, wearing a sad smile. "My dearly beloved, I can understand your grief. But you belong to the race of the immortals who live in the mountains and valleys. My natural element is the ocean and if I stay away too long, I will die of nostalgia.

You cannot follow me into my kingdom. You would drown. So we must separate. I will take fifty of our children with me into the ocean regions, and you can keep the other fifty with you in the mountain forests from where you came. We will divide the country so that it can be efficiently administered. Those who live in the highlands and those who live in the sea will always support each other. In this way we can live united forever."

The sons who followed Lac Long Quan to his kingdom became the ancestors of the Vietnamese people, with full rights to the coastal plains for all time. Those who accompanied Au Co gave birth to other diverse ethnic groups—the Muong, Tay, Hmong—and they live in the mountains to this day. The oldest of the children was appointed king, and he mounted the throne with the name of Huong Vong. Eighteen other kings succeeded him and continued this legendary dynasty.

16

The Two Genies and the Princess

The eighteenth King Huong Vuong, they say, had only one daughter, but what a daughter! Named My Nuong, she was more beautiful, more intelligent, and more virtuous than any other princess the world had ever known. Those who met her could not take their eyes off her. Those who heard her speak fell silent with admiration. It is hardly astonishing that when she was old enough to marry, her father decided to find her a worthy husband. Messengers went out to the four corners of the kingdom to announce the news, and soon dozens of suitors formed a queue in front of the palace in the twofold hope of pleasing the king and winning the young woman's heart. Great writers, virtuoso musicians, worthy warriors, famous astrologers, the most attractive and talented men in the kingdom, were all gathered in the one spot. But when the father and his daughter leisurely examined them all from the highest tower in the palace, one after the other, there was a problem. None of the candidates found favor in their eyes.

Suddenly two young men appeared who were far superior to all the others. They introduced themselves as Son Tinh, the genie of the mountains, and Thuy Tinh, the genie of the seas. Both were madly in love with the princess. One had seen her walking by the seaside, while the other had noticed her picnicking in a bamboo grove. And they had ways of supporting their case! Thuy Tinh could cast spells in a loud voice to summon the rain and lightning to beat against the fields. A violent storm erupted and the sky, which had been absolutely clear until then, instantly turned as black as ink. Whirlpools became typhoons and rivers overflowed their beds, transforming the fields into swamps, and thunderbolts smashed against the trees with such force that their roots were laid bare. Then it was Son Tinh's turn to show what he could do. Striking his magic wand against the ground, he created powerful winds that drove the clouds away in a second. The rain ceased, the grass became green again, and the world seemed to be reborn. The sun sparkled, casting its golden rays into the sweet pure air, and the birds sang, releasing their trills with a new found gaiety.

The king was confused. How the devil could he choose between these two exceptional suitors? It seemed impossible. So he declared, "You are both equally powerful. Either one of you would be a truly remarkable son-in-law from every point of view. I see no other way but to organize a test to decide between you. The first to bring me a hundred cakes of glutinous rice, two hundred *banh chung*, an elephant with nine tusks, a rooster with nine spurs, and a horse with nine red manes, will win the hand of the princess."

Son Tinh owned a magical book, which Thuy Tinh had given him, that granted its owner anything he wished for. The very next morning he returned to the palace, carrying the foods the king had asked for on gold and silver plates, and followed by the required animals one after the other. The king declared himself satisfied and the mountain genie led his promised bride away to live in a most beautiful palace located on the highest peak of the highest mountain. On the afternoon of that same day, the genie of the waters, who had had a little bit more difficulty in finding the presents demanded by the king, presented himself at the palace. When he learned that his brother had already left with the woman he loved, Thuy Tinh became violently angry. He sent an army of dragons and leeches to attack the world, and unleashing hurricanes and tempests, shook the earth to its foundations, before ordering the floods to cut off all the roads, swamp the fields, and cover the houses up to their roofs. The sky was dark and soon there was not a single piece of land that had not been submerged by devastating floods.

Son Tinh refused to allow his brother to behave in this way and he reacted as quickly as a flash of lightning. By raising new hills and moving mountains about, he stemmed the floods with the help of people who did their best to assist him. Bears and tigers also shared in building dams and protecting the plains and forests. Fighting relentlessly, Son Tinh saved entire communities from drowning.

The struggle continued for several months. It was impossible to tell how many bodies were buried beneath the water and the mud. Then one fine day the waters retreated, and after counting the casualties inflicted on both sides, it was decided that Thuy Tinh had lost. He had failed to fulfill his vow to destroy the world.

His resentment remained, however. Ever since then, at the same time each year—during the sixth and seventh months of the lunar calendar—the monsoons return, accompanied by a series of flooding rains and typhoons, from which the Vietnamese people must protect themselves as best they can. "The genies are fighting over the hand of the princess again," they regularly tell each other.

17
The Kingdom of the Immortals

Over six hundred years ago, during the Tran dynasty, there was a man called Tu Thuc. The son of a mandarin and the successful graduate of the imperial examinations at the age of twenty, he was quickly appointed to serve in the north. Near his residence was an old pagoda, celebrated throughout the region for the splendid peony tree that grew in its garden. In the first month of each lunar year, when the flowers bloomed profusely, large numbers of the faithful flocked to the pagoda to honor the Buddha, placing their offerings on the altar and admiring the blossoms. The celebration was known as the Peony Festival.

At that time the king strongly supported Buddhism, and the religious institutions followed the rules by which they had been established, applying those same rules to all who entered their precincts. To preserve the peony tree, they had decided that anyone who picked one of its flowers would be heavily fined—and, if they didn't have enough money, would be held captive and required to work off their debt. Now it so happened that one day a beautiful young girl, who would have been no older than sixteen, came to the festival at the pagoda. Knowing nothing of the rule, she bent down and picked a peony. She was immediately seized and asked to pay the fine. Not having brought any money with her, the guardians would not let her leave the pagoda unless her parents came and paid the proper amount. They even tied her to a pillar to make sure that she would not run away.

It was at that moment Tu Thuc intervened. Having only recently been appointed to his position, he had taken the opportunity to come incognito, without any escorts, without his palanquin, and without having been announced. It was difficult under those circumstances to exercise his authority. Wanting to save the young girl from her sad fate but not having the necessary amount of money with him, he took off his brocade robe and exchanged it for the youngster's freedom. She was overwhelmingly grateful. Observing her incomparable beauty, he awkwardly asked her about her origins. She replied, more or less, that she did not come from this region. Blushing, she said that she came from the same district where Tu Thuc grew up. Delighted, he chatted with her as if they were old friends. They were so happy together that it was only with the greatest of difficulty they finally took their leave. The young girl made the mandarin promise he would visit her whenever he returned to his own region.

Tu Thuc's noble action at the Peony Festival eventually became widely known and everyone praised his conduct. Unfortunately, the young man was much less respected by his superiors. Contrary to the usual practice, he refused to abase himself and flatter them, and he was openly adverse to honors and politics. Music and fine wine were his only interests. He loved nothing more than wandering through the most scenic places in the region, composing poetry. Neglecting his responsibilities and the tasks with which he was charged, he committed one fault after another, and in due time came to understand that he was not made for such a career. He hung the official stamp by its cords above the door as an indication of his having resigned. "Why should I be a prisoner of these circles of power and ambition for the sake of the few measures of rice that serve as my salary?" he thought to himself.

He decided to return to his homeland, where he could abandon himself to his passions: walking and searching for beautiful scenery, the springs and grottos that had always enchanted him, taking with him a calabash of wine, a guitar, and several sheets of paper to write down his poems. Jade Mountain, the Lake of the Heavenly Mirror, the Perfumed River—he visited them all and described them in fine verse. The memory of the young woman he had saved was continually in his heart and mind, but he felt that it would be impossible to find her.

One morning, when he awoke particularly early, he looked out to sea from the rocky plateau where he had made his home and spied a shining white island shaped like an opened lotus. Enchanted, he took a boat across to it and discovered the entrance to a grotto. The fresh flowers and the fragrant newly cut grass pleased him, and a mysterious bright radiance drew him further in. He followed the path forward and had scarcely taken more than a few steps when he felt the rocky walls close behind him. There was no other alternative but to grope his way forward, guided by the tiny light. When he reached the other end, he saw that he had reached the foot of a mountain covered by the purest white clouds. Helped by a series of crevices and breaks in the rocks, he began climbing. The further he climbed, the sweeter the air seemed to be and the easier the path.

Once he reached the summit, he was surprised to see a vast palace made of marble and carved rock, decorated with gold ornamentation, and surrounded by a garden of the rarest plants. The sun shone radiantly on the trees' luxuriant foliage, while a river of the purest water sang a limpid song. Two young servant women, dressed in robes that shimmered from blue to green, emerged from the palace. On seeing him, one of them shouted, "Behold, the young bridegroom has come!" They both rushed inside the palace to announce his arrival before reemerging to lead him through a lacquered door and down a corridor covered in velvet, to a fairy dressed in white silk. She invited him to sit down.

"I know your love for traveling, for lakes and forests," she said with a smile. "You know them better than anyone else. But the places you have discovered today are very different. Do you have any idea where you are?"

"Not at all," Tu Thuc declared. "I had never thought that there could be anywhere as beautiful as this. And I can scarcely believe that this is real."

"There is nothing to be astonished about," replied the fairy. "No other human being has ever been able to come here. You are in the sixth of the thirty-six grottos in the kingdom of the immortals. We sail across all the seas and never set foot on land. The island is shaped by the winds, the rain, and the sea, and moves as they wish. I am the queen, and in honor of your pure soul, I would like to offer you our hospitality. I am happy to welcome you, knowing too that you are about to meet an old friend."

Turning towards her servants, the fairy nodded. They silently retired, then a young woman of exquisite beauty made her entrance. Stunned, Tu Thuc recognized the young maiden he had rescued at the pagoda. "Here is my daughter, Giang Huong, 'scarlet incense.' When she descended to earth to help at the Peony Festival, she unknowingly committed an offense that put her in a very difficult position. You were courteous and discrete in the way you assisted her. Since that time, you have never stopped searching for her. Heaven has brought you together for a second time, and I have decided to allow you to unite your destinies. If you both agree." Filled with joy, Tu Thuc reached out and the young girl took his hand. All the fairies were invited to the wedding, and in honor of the day all the flowers blossomed at the same time and the birds sang in harmony.

Weeks flew by as if they were hours, and three years quickly passed in the fairy kingdom—three years of peace and happiness for the couple, who were truly blessed. Tu Thuc devoted all his time to walking and to poetry, while his wife listened and took good care of him. But at the end of those three years, the young man felt profoundly nostalgic. Day after day, he became more and more indifferent to the flowing waters and the supernatural scenery. And the nights, which had previously been so sweet, now seemed empty. He lay awake at night, waiting for the roosters to crow, as used to happen in his village. Melancholy slowly took possession of his soul, and he lost his taste for life.

Taking his courage in both hands, he revealed his feelings to his wife. "My dearly beloved, I have not seen my family for three years, or my friends. They might be worried about me. Perhaps they think I am dead. I would like to visit them and reassure everyone, and to see the places of my childhood again because I miss them enormously. Will you allow me to go? I will be away for a few weeks at the most, perhaps two months. Then I will return and never leave you again, I promise." Giang Hong was silent for a few moments, and then she replied slowly, weighing each of her words. "If that is what you want, I cannot stop you. However I fear that you are wrong about your return. Everything changes in the world of mortals, and your quest may seem to be hollow. You are searching for the fire and the vitality of your past. What if only the ashes remain?"

Tu Thuc, overjoyed by the prospect of being among his own people for a while, scarcely listened to her warning. And when she confided her distress to her mother, the queen thoughtfully observed, "I did not think that he was still attached to the shadows and dust of the world. It does not matter—he has made his choice and we must let him go."

A few days later, the fairies gathered to honor Tu Thuc and to wish him farewell. Weeping, he embraced his wife and vainly tried to comfort her, assuring Giang Hong that he would soon return. The queen created a magical chariot and asked the young man to mount it. A light breeze blew, the wonderful scenes passed quickly by, and in a few seconds Tu Thuc was back in his own village. He recognized the rocky mountain summits, the bamboo hedges, and the clear water where he had bathed as a child—none of that had changed. But everything else—the streets, the houses, the faces of the people—they were all completely different. And when he introduced himself to one person and then another, they were all perplexed. His name meant absolutely nothing to them. Finally, however, a very shaky old man who held the village's memories at last recalled, "I heard tell, when I was still a small boy, that an ancestor of mine bearing that name left his position and went into the mountains to compose poetry, and that he must have fallen into a ravine because no one ever heard of him again. That was at least three centuries ago."

Tu Thuc felt an icy blast pass across his heart. Recalling his beloved's words about the futility of the material world, he sighed and tried to return to the magic chariot. But it had evaporated, as if it were made of clouds. He understood too late that farewell had in fact become goodbye forever.

Some time later, he set out alone to wander as he used to do among the mountains and rivers. No one knows whether he perished or if the road to the kingdom of the immortals opened itself to him again.

18
The Princess and the Fisherman

This is a story—it happened a very long time ago—about the daughter of a very senior mandarin. Endowed with all the graces, she was named My Nuong, which means "beautiful child." Like all young girls of high rank, she lived a reclusive life in the women's quarters located in a high tower of the palace. Constantly surrounded by only her servants, she had no visitors apart from her parents. Her room was sumptuously furnished and her cupboard was filled with clothes made of the finest silk, but she cared for neither one nor the other. Most of the time she sat by the window, embroidering or reading books of poetry. Sometimes she paused to look at the river that ran into the distance, and she dreamed of following its silvery waters to far-off places and of the people she might meet there.

Every day a fisherman's small boat would glide across the calm waters. The man, Truong Chi, was very poor. He often sang, but as he was so far away, My Nuong could not see his face and could scarcely distinguish his movements. Yet she could hear his voice, rising from the river to where she was. He had a beautiful voice and the words of his songs were very sad. This was the only contact the young girl ever had with the outside world, apart from those times when she had lifted the curtain of her palanquin on the few occasions when her father allowed her to leave the palace, escorted by thousands of the mandarin's best guards.

One day, however, the fisherman did not come to the river. My Nuong was surprised to find herself waiting for him until evening fell. During the following days, she looked in vain for his return. She hardly slept at night and lost her appetite. Summoned in haste, the physicians were unable to determine the cause of her illness, and her parents began to despair, when the young girl suddenly recovered. The fisherman had returned, singing again on his boat.

Advised by a servant that My Nuong was attached to the fisherman's singing, the mandarin called him and brought him before the girl. At one glance, all the vague daydreams aroused by his songs came to an end. Truong Chi was ugly and dressed in rags. He had nothing about him of the Prince Charming My Nuong often imagined. She forgot about him and found her peace of mind once more. However the poor fisherman suffered a fatal blow the moment he saw My Nuong. He returned to the river but, as time passed, he was never able to forget the young lady's beauty or disdain. Consumed by a hopeless love, he died in silence, carrying his secret with him.

Some years later, a flood caused the fisherman's family to dig up his remains and move them to another grave. There was nothing in his coffin but a strange translucent stone, which they used as an ornament on their boat. A passing craftsman noticed this unusual stone and bought it from them. He carved the stone into an exquisite teacup.

My Nuong's mandarin father acquired the cup when he had wind of a remarkable phenomenon. Each time one poured tea into the cup, an image of a fisherman in a boat appeared, slowly sailing around the inside and singing,

> *Since our hearts*
> *will never meet in his world*
> *May our souls be united forever*
> *in the world to come.*

One day in autumn, My Nuong poured a little tea into the cup. The image of the fisherman appeared. They looked at each other. The young girl remembered him. She wept.

A tear fell into the cup, which immediately melted away.